Tess hated to disappoint anyone. Would she disappoint Tom, Erin, her parents, and God all in one week?

AFTER A FEW BUMPY HOURS ON THE BUS, TESS HAD ALMOST forgotten about her problem.

She and Erin had squeezed together on a bench near the back of the bus.

"Did you talk with your parents about the ride to church?" Erin asked.

"Yes," Tess said. She rushed to change the subject, not wanting to trouble her friend. "I hate these greasy diesel fumes. On the way home let's sit near the front."

Erin plugged her nose before nodding in agreement and said nothing else about getting to church.

Tess checked her watch. "How long till we get there?"

"Not long at all," Erin said. "I'm so excited! Our first mission trip! I hope it goes okay."

What could go wrong?

Secret Sisters: (se´-krit sis´-terz) n. Two friends who choose each other to be everything a real sister should be: loyal and loving. They share with and help each other no matter what!

Secret ✳ Sisters

Indian Summer

Sandra Byrd

WATERBROOK
PRESS

INDIAN SUMMER
PUBLISHED BY WATERBROOK PRESS
2375 Telstar Drive, Suite 160
Colorado Springs, Colorado 80920
A division of Random House, Inc.

Scriptures in the Secret Sisters series are quoted from the *International Children's Bible, New Century Version,* copyright © 1986, 1988 by Word Publishing, Nashville, TN 37214. Used by permission.

The characters and events in this book are fictional, and any resemblance to actual persons or events is coincidental.

ISBN 1-57856-270-8

Published in association with the literary agency of Janet Kobobel Grant, Books & Such, 3093 Maiden Lane, Altadena, CA 91001.

Printed in the United States of America
2000—First Edition

10 9 8 7 6 5 4 3 2 1

To honor my Lord,
the Alpha and Omega of everything

one

Be Brave

Saturday Night, August 2

Twelve-year-old Tess Thomas fidgeted in the third row—
the closest she had ever sat to the front in the church's
classroom. The smell of someone's rotting sneakers turned
her nervous stomach.

Come on, Tess, you want to do this, she reminded herself. *No one is forcing you.* She tucked her dark brown hair
behind her ears and tried to focus on Pastor Jack, who was
speaking at the front of the room.

"Finally, on the last day of our trip, we'll have a river
baptism ceremony during which some of you will publicly
commit your lives to Christ." Jack snapped shut his Bible.
"If you haven't signed up, tonight is your last chance. See
you bright and early tomorrow."

Stay calm! Tess breathed so fast she felt dizzy. Her heart
pounded a rhythm in her ears, and she didn't hear one
word of the closing prayer besides "amen."

Afterward, Tess reached for Erin's hand. "Come on." She
tugged on the arm of her best friend and Secret Sister.

"Come on where?" Erin's forehead wrinkled.

"I thought you said you were going to get baptized, too."

"No," Erin said. "I was thinking about it. But when I talked it over with my brothers last night, we decided we wanted to do it together, all at once. And Josh isn't old enough yet."

"Oh." Erin's hand practically slid out of Tess's moist palm as Tess loosened her grip.

"You could do it when we do, maybe next year." Erin twirled a piece of her blond hair in her fingers. "It won't be in the river though. Probably at the community pool."

Tess hadn't taken her eyes off Pastor Jack. "Thanks, but I prayed about it, and I really feel like I'm supposed to do it now." She turned toward Erin. "I'm scared, but I'm excited, too!"

Erin nodded.

Tess frowned. "Why would God tell me yes now, but not you? I mean, since I became a Christian last year, we've done everything together."

"We don't do the church nursery together," Erin reminded her. "'Cause I'm no good with kids." Her eyes lowered. "Last time I tried, they all cried. I'm afraid to even baby-sit."

Tess patted her friend's arm. "That happened a long time ago."

"It doesn't seem so long ago to me," Erin said.

Tess noticed Pastor Jack packing up his notes. "Wait for me, okay, Erin?" She wiped her palms on her shorts and made her way toward the front. Most of the other kids were on their way home to prepare for tomorrow's early morning bus ride. As they left, the noise hustled out with them. The quiet room made her voice seem even louder. "Pastor Jack?"

Pastor Jack stood alone now. He turned around. "Hi, Tess."

"I, uh, I know I haven't talked to you about this yet, but I'd really like to be baptized this week. Is that okay?"

"Sure, Tess. The other three have filled out their worksheets and met with me. How about if I give you the baptism material now, and we meet Friday at the Navajo reservation to go over your questionnaire? After talking, if we feel that you're not ready, we won't go through with it."

Tess's smile froze.

"I'm sure there won't be a problem," Jack continued.

Tess nodded.

"The kids who will be baptized asked their parents to come along this week," Pastor Jack continued. "I know your parents aren't Christians, but would they like to be there? I could arrange something."

Her parents go on the trip? Watch her be baptized? Uh-uh. "No thanks," Tess said. "I don't think they would be interested."

Jack's face softened as he reached into his briefcase and handed her a packet.

"We'll get together on Friday, and if all goes well, you can be baptized on Saturday."

Tess nodded. "All right." She slipped the packet into her notebook. "I'll see you tomorrow."

"See you tomorrow."

Tess turned and walked back toward the refreshment table where Erin sipped from a can of 7UP. "I think I need something cold to drink, too!" Tess felt giddy with happiness. She snagged a Coke from the table but didn't open it.

"So how did it go?" Erin moved close to Tess.

"Great! I have to fill out these papers on what baptism

means and why I want to do it, and then I can be baptized on Saturday. We're going to have so much fun. A whole week away together—on an Indian reservation. And now this, too!"

"It's so cool. Totally exciting." Erin tossed her empty can into the recycling bin and took out a stick of Secret Sisters gum. They had decided always to chew the same kind of gum; that way, even when they were apart, they would be doing something together.

Erin popped the gum into her mouth and shot the wrapper into the garbage. "But I'm surprised your parents said baptism was okay. I know they felt weird about your going with the church for a whole week."

Tess's smile broke, and her stomach turned even though the kid with the rotting sneakers had long since left the room. "Well, I haven't told them yet."

Erin's mouth opened, but no words came out.

"I only just made the decision!" Tess rushed in. "I mean, I've hardly had any time to talk to them, with the baby crying a lot. Then my brother's birthday was yesterday, and I didn't want to distract them from that." She looked at Erin. "I know I have to tell them. I *want* to tell them."

"Uh-huh," Erin said. "Sounds like t-r-o-u-b-l-e to me." She looked at the clock above the refreshment table. "We can talk more about this later. My mom will be here in five minutes to pick us up."

Tess adjusted her notebook and can of pop. "Let's go then!" she said, eager to change the subject.

"Wait!" Erin grabbed her arm. Except for the two of them, the room was empty, and Erin's voice echoed off the gray walls. "I have to talk with you about something important before we get in the car with my mom."

two

Big News

Saturday Night, August 2

"Is something the matter?" Tess asked.

"It's about my family—and me." Erin looked up at the clock, which stared down at them like a large, white eye. "I guess I'd better tell you on the way. I don't want my mom to wait."

Erin headed out the door and paused for Tess to catch up with her. Just then, a woman stopped them in the hall.

"Tess," she said, "may I talk with you for a minute?"

Tess glanced at Erin. They had just a few minutes before Erin's mom was going to be there, but what could Tess say?

"Sure." Tess stepped to the side of the hall, where Mrs. Fye waited. Mrs. Fye worked in children's ministry, and Tess baby-sat for her sometimes too.

"I planned to talk with you after church tomorrow, but I just realized that you won't be here. You'll be on the mission trip to the Navajo reservation, won't you?"

"Yes," Tess said.

"I wondered if you're still planning to work with the nursery or preschool kids one Sunday a month this fall,"

Mrs. Fye continued. "You do such a good job; many parents comment on how much they like you. We would love to keep you."

Out of the corner of her eye, Tess caught a sharp look from Erin. She was shaking her head no. Why would Erin care if Tess worked with the kids?

"I think it would be fine," Tess said. "Can I tell you for sure next week?"

"Yes," Mrs. Fye said. "But no later because I'd like to set up all the workers before September. I hope you'll say yes." She smiled and walked down the hall.

Erin checked her watch. "We had better get moving."

"Why did you shake your head at me?" Tess asked. "Are you mad because we're not working together, 'cause you're not comfortable with little kids?"

"No," Erin said. "It's about what I have to tell you. But I don't want to blab it all over the hall where just anyone can hear me. Let's sit on the bench by the front door."

Finally they reached the bench. "Okay, enough with the mystery, what's going on?" Tess said.

"My family and I aren't coming to church anymore."

"*What?*" Tess's voice boomed so loud several people nearby stopped chatting to stare. "Sorry." Tess lowered her voice. "What do you mean?"

"I mean, we're going to church, but we're not going to this one. For a while." Erin sighed and looked out the window, then back at Tess. "You know my grandpa's been sick with cancer, right?"

"Yeah." Tess nodded. "Is he okay?"

"I don't know for sure," Erin said. "It seems like it. But he's having chemotherapy, and he's really weak. My grandma thinks it would be really good for him to go to church, but she's pretty tired out from doing a lot of stuff at the ranch since he's been sick. So my mom and dad decided today that we would spend every Sunday with them. You know, take them to their own church, eat dinner with them, and help around the ranch, doing stuff my grandpa can't do right now. Just until he's feeling stronger. Maybe Christmas or something."

"Oh." Tess picked at a corner of her notebook, and a shred of paper flittered to the floor. "I see why you didn't want me to promise to help out with the kids."

"It means we can't take you to church for a while," Erin said. "My mom can help you find another ride. After she's done making some calls for my grandpa, that is. He's starting a new treatment."

"No," Tess said. The last thing she wanted was to add another burden to Erin's mom, who already had been so nice to Tess, taking her practically everywhere for almost a year. "My mom and dad probably will drive me."

Erin sighed with relief. "Do you think so? That would be great."

Tess smiled weakly. The truth was, her mom and dad probably weren't going to be in a huge, hopping hurry to get dressed early on Sundays to take her to church. Sometimes her dad went hiking, and that left only her mom to care for Tess's one-month-old sister and Tyler, her nine-year-old brother. But Tess didn't want to worry Erin or make her think that Tess's parents were uncooperative.

"Here's my mom." Erin stood up, and the girls walked outside, where Erin's older brother Tom already waited. Tess smiled shyly at him, and her heart squeezed out an extra beat. Tom didn't flash his usual dimpled grin. Instead, he clutched a thick leader's notebook and nodded hello.

"Hi, girls," Erin's mother said as they climbed into the dusty Suburban. "Did you have a good time?"

"Yes!" Erin said. "I can't wait till tomorrow. This trip is going to be so fun. And Tess is going to be baptized."

"That's wonderful!" Erin mother said. "Congratulations, Tess. This is a really important week, isn't it? Look." She pointed at her arm. "I have goose bumps just thinking about your being baptized!"

Tess looked down at her own arm, freckled with goose bumps as well. "Me, too."

Tom, who was sitting in the front passenger seat, said nothing, concentrating on the now open notebook in front of him. He was the mission's student leader this year. His jaw clenched and released several times as he scanned his papers.

"How's the mission plan going?" Tess looked at his face. He had such nice eyes.

"All right, I guess. There's so much to remember and do. Pastor Jack is expecting a lot from me. And next year we're going to Mexico for short-term missions, so I want to make sure we really do a good job. That way we'll be ready for the bigger trip to Mexico."

"You've done a terrific job preparing. You can do it," his mother reassured.

"It's really hard. What if something goes wrong? I shouldn't have agreed to be in charge."

Before Tess could stop the words, she spoke up. "You never seemed like the kind of person who was afraid to try something hard." Fearing she had gone too far, she tacked a smile onto the end of the sentence.

Tom looked right in her eyes. Tess didn't look away.

Then he half smiled. "Yeah, well." He turned back around and faced front again.

"What's your job?" Mrs. Janssen asked Erin.

"Tess and I are going to cut out the craft materials and help out in the kitchen."

"Fun!"

"Yeah, fun," Erin agreed. "And we have parties and projects planned."

And it will be low stress, Tess thought. *Plenty of time to work on my baptism questions.*

She watched the streetlights begin to flicker on. It was growing late, and she hadn't put even one thing into her suitcase. "I still have to pack," she said.

"Don't forget to pack me a Secret Sisters snack bag," Erin reminded her with a giggle.

Tess giggled back. Erin and her food. Walking-stick-thin Erin never forgot a snack. "I didn't forget. I have some cool stuff for you."

"And me for you," Erin said. Whenever they went on a field trip or some other bus ride, each girl packed a snack bag for the other. They put in some healthy lunch stuff but also secret treats. That way each of them had a surprise to enjoy on the trip. As Secret Sisters, they chose to be everything to each other a sister should be.

Mrs. Janssen pulled her car up to the Thomases' house. "Tess," she said as Tess gathered her things, "did Erin tell you about church when you get back from the trip? That we won't be able to drive you for a few months?"

"Yes, I understand."

"I'm sorry," Mrs. Janssen said. "May I help you find a ride?"

"No thanks," Tess said in a rush.

"I figured your parents would probably do it." Mrs. Janssen smiled. "If I bump into your mom this week, I'll tell her I can take you again starting after Christmas."

Bump into her mom this week? *I guess I'll have to tell Mom and Dad tonight. As if I don't have enough on my mind.* She would tell her parents about needing a ride first, before breaking the news about baptism.

"See you tomorrow morning." Tess opened the car door. Erin and Mrs. Janssen waved, but Tom was buried in his papers, scribbling last-minute notes.

Tess slammed the Suburban's door and took as much time as possible walking up to her house.

three

A Decision

Saturday Night, August 2

Two grasshoppers leaped into the brittle grass as Tess walked up the front path. The doorknob had baked in the Arizona sun all day, and she burned her hand as she twisted the knob. Even though it was evening, the day wouldn't cool off to less than ninety degrees until well after midnight.

Tess stepped into the foyer, kicking off her shoes. "Anybody here?" she called down the hallway, walking toward the family room.

"We're all in here, honey," her mother called back.

Tess reached the family room and plopped down on the couch next to her mother.

"Hi, goo-goo girl." Tess kissed her baby sister Tara's forehead. Tess breathed in the sweet, powdery smell of the baby's head. Tara's eyes stayed closed, her little eyelashes fanning out on her chubby, pink cheeks.

"Say, old chum, I thought *you* were the goo-goo girl," her nine-year-old brother, Tyler, teased.

"And I thought when you turned nine you would drop

that goofy fake British accent," Tess teased back. Tyler wanted to be a detective with Scotland Yard when he grew up.

"Never!" he said. "I'm going to my room." The beeps and screeches of his Game Boy trailed behind him.

"So how was your meeting?" her mother asked.

"It was good," Tess said. *So what should I tell them first? Good news.* "Since we're some of the youngest in the group, Erin and I have easy, really fun jobs. We're going to have a great time."

"Wonderful!" her mother said.

"I can't wait. I was worried I would get something hard. Tom is totally stressed out. He's in charge. He's afraid he'll mess up, and something will go really wrong."

"Hi, cupcake. How's my girl?" Tess's dad said as he walked into the room with a bowl of ice cream. He spooned some into his mouth and swallowed before continuing. "Erin's parents will pick you up tomorrow morning, right?"

"Yes." Tess settled into the couch. "Can I hold the baby?"

Her mother handed over the baby, and Tess snuggled the sleeping girl.

Tess's breathing grew fast and shallow. "But about Erin's parents…" She glanced at her mother then her father and back to her mother again. "We need to talk about something. Right away."

Her dad snapped off the television set. "What is it?" He set down his ice cream on the table beside his La-Z-Boy chair.

"Well, remember Erin told you that her grandpa was sick?"

Her mother's eyes flew open wide. "He didn't die, did he?"

"No, no. It's just that he wants to keep going to church, and their grandma is too weak to push the wheelchair and carry everything. She needs help on the ranch, too."

Tess looked down at her sister as Tara whimpered. *Please, Tara, don't cry now. Let me finish.*

"Seems reasonable," her dad said. "So what's the problem?"

Tess took a deep breath. "They'll be going to Gilbert on Sundays, where her grandparents live. So they won't be able to take me to church for a while. At least a couple of months. I wondered if you guys could give me a ride."

Tara squirmed a little but didn't cry. Tess's mother said nothing. Then her dad finally spoke. "I don't know, Tess. I'm not real excited about your being in a strange church by yourself every week. It's a little different when you're there with Erin and her family."

"It's not strange. And you could come with me," Tess said.

Her dad settled back. "Tess, I'm starting to understand how you feel about Jesus. But I've gone to your church a couple of times and have felt totally out of place. It's not for me. Maybe you're getting a little too involved with this church stuff."

Her parents looked at one another before her mother spoke up. "We have a lot going on with the baby now. Maybe this would be a good time for you to take a break from church. You could spend some time on Sunday mornings hiking with your dad. You haven't done that for quite a while."

"But I like church," Tess insisted. "I want to go." Tara raised a fist in her sleep, and Tess jostled her, trying to keep her asleep.

"I don't know. After all," her father said, "you can pray and read the Bible at home. I don't like your being there alone."

Tess's heart flip-flopped; she looked straight down instead of at her parents and said nothing.

"You won't be here this Sunday, so we don't have to decide right now," her mother said.

Just then Tara's face grew tight and then bright red. She burst out crying.

"I'll take her," her mother said. "She's hungry. Why don't you finish packing, and I'll come in and check on you in a little bit?" Her mom took the baby without waiting for an answer and, cooing over the little girl, walked from the room. Tess's dad clicked the television back on and picked up his melting ice cream.

Tess's heart didn't flip-flop anymore. It lay flat and still inside her. *I guess this conversation is over.* Tess walked down the hall to her room.

She flicked on the light, and the CD player kicked in at the same time; her dad had wired them all together. She tapped some fish food into Goldy's bowl.

"That'll last you."

After yanking her suitcase out of the closet, she tossed in some clothes. T-shirts, sleeveless shirts, some shorts. Shoes. Bible. Lemon Heads.

Don't forget to make Erin's Secret Sister snack bag, she reminded herself.

Bible. Hairbrush. Glitter lip gloss.

She looked at her bathing suit. She had left it on the doorknob to her room to drip dry. *Too involved with this church stuff? I don't think they're going to be thrilled about my getting baptized.*

She pictured her dad clicking on the television, ending their conversation. *I know I have to tell them about baptism, and I will. But not right now. One major problem tonight is enough.*

After staring at the bathing suit for a good two or three minutes, she walked over and unlooped it from the doorknob. Completely dry, it crinkled crisply and smelled of dried chlorine from the backyard pool. *I might need the bathing suit to wear under the baptismal robe.*

She stuffed the suit into the bottom of her suitcase under a pair of shorts.

four

Big Embarrassment

Sunday, August 3

Trying to get ready the next morning, Tess didn't have a second to talk to her parents about baptism. The baby was crying, and her dad was in a hurry to go hiking with his boss, Vince. After a few bumpy hours on the bus, Tess had almost forgotten about her problem.

She and Erin had squeezed together on a bench near the back of the bus.

"Did you talk with your parents about the ride to church?" Erin asked.

"Yes," Tess said. She rushed to change the subject, not wanting to trouble her friend. "I hate these greasy diesel fumes. On the way home let's sit near the front."

Erin plugged her nose before nodding in agreement and said nothing else about getting to church.

Tess checked her watch. "How long till we get there?"

"Not long at all," Erin said. "I'm so excited! Our first mission trip! I hope it goes okay."

"What could go wrong? The parties sound fun, too, especially the backwards party." Tess unzipped her backpack and pulled out the brown paper bag she had decorated with stickers the night before. "Want to open our Secret Sisters snack bags? I hope you like what I packed."

Erin handed over her bag. She had painted it with watercolors in American Indian designs.

Tess sighed. "Now I know why you're in charge of art. Yours is so much better than mine."

Erin swatted at her. "Get lost. Just open it up and see what you think."

Tess unrolled the top of her bag. "Lemon Heads, of course. Yum. A bottle of lemonade. Lemon cookies. I'm starting to catch a theme here." She giggled. "You're not saying I'm sour, are you?"

"Nope." Erin unrolled her bag top. "All right, Ding Dongs." She smiled at her friend. "You're not calling me a ding-dong, are you?"

Tess giggled again. "Well…"

Erin laughed, too, and they each unwrapped something to eat.

"Hey," an older guy called from the front of the bus. "Want to play twenty questions?"

"Yeah!" most of the kids called back.

"I'm thinking of a thing," he started.

"Is it alive?"

"Nope."

"Is there one in Arizona?"

"Nope."

"Is there one on earth?"

Two girls going into ninth grade started to laugh at that person's question. Tess recognized one of them as Shannon, who was pretty and in charge a lot of the time.

After several more questions, someone guessed correctly, "A moonrock!"

Tess wrapped her snack bag back up. *I should play. Just to be part of things with everyone else.* She was going to offer an idea when Shannon jumped in.

"I'm thinking of a person," Shannon announced.

After a while, they had narrowed it down to one of the twelve disciples. It wasn't Peter or John.

Go ahead, take a guess. Tess cleared her throat. "Is it Paul?"

Erin sucked in her breath, and the entire bus grew quiet.

"Don't you know that Paul wasn't one of the original twelve disciples?!" Shannon shouted.

Tess sank into her seat like a worm into quicksand. Her heart was on fire with shame. Ten painfully silent seconds ticked by before the guessing started again. From the front of the bus, Tom looked at her with sympathy as Shannon tugged on his sleeve.

I don't want your sympathy, Tess thought and looked away.

"It's okay," Erin whispered. "I'll bet a lot of other people thought that, people who have been Christians lots longer than you."

Tess nodded but didn't look up, afraid tears would spill onto her cheeks and embarrass her even more. She didn't feel like talking to Erin or anyone right now. Instead, she took out her notebook and pretended to work on her baptism questions.

Why did I even try? Now I've embarrassed not only myself but also Erin and Tom.

She swallowed the lump in her throat and doodled on

the page. Maybe Erin would think Tess was working and wouldn't talk with her right now.

Tess took out the baptism questions from the back of her notebook. *Maybe I'm not ready to be baptized. Maybe I have to know a lot more.*

"What are you doing?" Erin tried to peek at the paper in front of Tess.

"Working on my questions."

Erin reached into her backpack and took out her Walkman and headphones. "I'm going to listen to music for a while, okay?"

"Okay." Tess looked out of the window as the dry desert landscape rolled by. They already had crossed the state line; she had seen the sign that read, "Welcome to New Mexico, Land of Enchantment." But it still looked like Arizona. Mile upon mile of parched earth baking in the sun, studded with spindly green sagebrush. The bushes clung to the hot earth with thin, fingerlike roots, tougher than they seemed. Inside the bus was hot, too, even with the windows all down.

"Hey, Tess." Melissa, the girl Tess worked with in the nursery, leaned across the aisle. "I just wondered if you were going to teach preschool next fall."

Tess flipped over a page in her notebook so she could keep her notes to herself. "I'm not sure."

"Oh. I know you like working with the kids, that's all. I do, too. I'm going to work in the preschool second hour. I wish we could be teachers at VBS this year instead of doing cleanup, don't you?"

"It's okay with me. I want to spend some time on these." Tess pointed to a sheet from the baptism questionnaire.

"Are you going to be baptized?"

"Yeah," Tess said. But inside she thought, *Maybe.* Even though she liked Melissa, Tess wasn't going to discuss her hesitancy with Melissa.

"Me, too!" Melissa said. "So of course my parents are here chaperoning. And they want to stand next to the river when I get baptized. Pastor Jack has someone who is going to stand by you during your Christian life do that. Are your parents here?" She looked toward the front of the bus where the parents sat.

"No," Tess said.

"Oh yeah, that's right." Melissa cast her glance away. "Sorry."

Neither girl said anything, and after a bit Melissa smiled awkwardly and turned away.

Tess stole a glance toward the front of the bus, where Tom sat. Shannon was trying to engage him in conversation, but he seemed more interested in his leader's notebook than in her constant chatter.

At least he's not thinking about my big mistake anymore. I hope.

Shannon caught Tess's eye and held her glance for a second before Tess looked away. Shannon didn't smile.

Tess slipped her notebook back into her backpack and opened her lemonade. She drank some and then screwed the cap back on and closed her eyes.

After what seemed like only a few minutes, Erin tapped Tess's shoulder. "Hey!" she said, pointing out the window. "We're here."

five

An Unexpected Change

Sunday Evening, August 3

"We're here?" Tess opened her eyes and looked out the window.

"We're in Shiprock." Erin leaned down to put her Walkman into her backpack.

Tess watched the low landscape roll by, flat and dry but broken here and there with mountains—brown sugar hills that looked like sandcastles on a beach, slightly crumbling into one another. Then the land grew gently wavy, like an ocean wave rippling underneath the earth's skin.

As the bus sped across a bridge, Tess stared down into churning river water. *Is that the river they baptize in?* Goose bumps fluttered across her skin again.

Pastor Jack stood up. "We'll pull into the mission church in just a few minutes. After we unload our backpacks and set up, we'll eat dinner and make plans for tomorrow."

The bus stopped in front of a church the color of bright pink birthday cake frosting. Tess and the others grabbed the gear and climbed off the bus. They stood around in front of the building, not sure what to do next.

Just then a young man with a thick shock of flat black hair strode out of the church. "Welcome!" He opened his arms and grabbed Pastor Jack in a big bear hug. Jack hugged him back, and they clapped one another on the shoulder.

"I'd like you to meet Pastor Peter Yazzi." Jack smiled at his friend as he introduced him to the crowd. "He's in charge of this church, and we'll be working under his direction this week."

Pastor Yazzi waved at the crowd, then led them into the church.

"Wow," Erin whispered as they hauled their stuff into the sanctuary.

Tess twirled to look around her. Glorious Navajo rugs draped the church walls; the big rug behind the pastor had three red crosses in the center with people of every shape and color woven around the border. The rest of the church was simple—chipped folding chairs, worn carpet. Tess stared at the Bibles and songbooks stacked in the corner. Most of the books were well used, with spines shredding.

"Let's get set up," Erin said. "Did you hear him say we could sleep in the Sunday-school rooms?"

Tess tore her gaze away from the amazing rugs. "No, but that's cool. Let's go."

They each grabbed their sleeping bags and backpacks and headed toward the hallway. Noah's ark paintings brightened the walls of the Sunday-school room they found. Old crates stood against the wall, tipping a little with their load of toys and supplies.

"Stay beside us," Melissa said.

"Thanks." Erin unrolled her sleeping bag next to Melissa's. Tess unrolled hers next to Erin's.

"It's nice and cool in here," Tess said. "Did you guys notice this church has five walls instead of four? And they're shaped kind of sideways or something."

"My mom said that's called a hogan." Melissa brushed her hair. "Navajos want their important buildings to have more than four walls."

Tess swallowed. "It's kind of like another country, isn't it?"

"Yeah." Melissa set down her brush. They all stared at one another in silence.

Just then Pastor Jack stuck his head into the room. "Tess, Erin, could you help in the kitchen?" He pointed to Melissa. "And you can go downstairs with your mother, Melissa. I have her rearranging the tables for VBS tomorrow."

"All right." Melissa took off downstairs.

Tess and Erin trekked down the hall, looking for the kitchen. They passed the sanctuary, where Tom stood with a small cluster of older kids from the youth group. VBS teachers, Tess guessed. Shannon, the twenty-questions girl from the bus, leaned on a pew right up front, looking sure and smooth. Tess made herself stop staring and followed Erin down the hall toward the spicy smell of cooking meat. Once in the small kitchen, Tess realized just how good the aroma was. She scanned the room and saw a dark brown stove and a scratched metal sink.

"Can we help?" Erin asked an older woman wearing a bright red skirt. The woman flipped big puffy things that looked like tortilla doughnuts in a huge pot of oil. Across the room was a large table heavy with bowlfuls of chopped tomatoes, whipped peaks of sour cream, and slivers of lettuce.

"I'm making fry bread for Navajo tacos," the woman answered. Her voice had a slight lilt, a little rhythm that made Tess think the lady's first language wasn't English. "Why don't one of you grate the cheese and one of you stir the beans?"

Erin went to a side table stacked with blocks of cheese. Tess stayed nearby to stir the beans.

"My name is Tess," she offered shyly.

The woman turned toward her. "My name is Eleanor."

Tess studied Eleanor's gentle face, the color of a lunch sack with the same kind of soft creases. Her deep black eyes matched her hair, which was dusted with gray and pulled back into a kind of bun at the nape of her neck.

"We're glad you could come and stay with us this week."

"Thanks for inviting us." Tess stirred the bubbling pot of beans faster, scraping the bottom to keep them from burning. "I hope we'll be good help."

"You will." Eleanor smiled. "Jesus likes helping hands. That's why I'm here tonight." She looked at the pot. "I think the beans are okay. Why don't you make sure the paper plates, forks, spoons, and everything are set out on the tables?"

Tess nodded and headed for the room where they would eat their meals. When she stepped inside, she saw that everything was ready to go. Then Tom and the group of teachers came into the room. Tom ran his hand through his hair, worry creeping across his face. He looked at Tess and smiled, heading in her direction.

"You're just who I want to see," he said.

"I am?" Tess answered, pleased. Out of the corner of her eye she saw Shannon watching her.

"Yes. Where's Erin?"

"In the kitchen. Do you want me to get her?"

Tom nodded. "Hurry."

What's up? Tess wondered. She ran into the kitchen and grabbed Erin. "Tom wants to see us. He said to hurry."

Erin set aside the grated cheese and wiped her hands on a paper towel. Then she followed Tess, who hurried back into the dining room. They sat down next to Tom.

"I have to change your jobs," he said.

"No problem," Tess said. "We can work the kitchen cleanup crew." Cleanup crew and party planning were what most of the other seventh and eighth graders were doing.

"No, I need two new teachers. We have five more kids coming, three boys and two girls. We can't have more than eight kids at a table."

"Teach?" Erin said. "As in, the kids?"

"Come on, Tess will help you. You'll be okay. It's important that everything go great, and you're the ones I trust most."

Tess swallowed hard. *Tess will help you?* Sure, she had worked in the nursery, and she had baby-sat. But she had never taught anything, let alone taught kids she never had met. Not to mention she didn't even know what she was supposed to teach them.

"Thanks. I knew I could count on you guys." Tom's old dimpled smile was back; he relaxed in his seat. Tess tried to rustle up a smile of her own for him. Erin said nothing.

"I'll meet you in the sanctuary after dinner and give you

the teaching manuals. You can stay up late tonight to look over tomorrow's lesson, and tomorrow night look over the next day's lesson. Just like that."

So much for having extra time to do the baptism questions.

Tom stood up and turned to leave. He stopped, snapped his fingers, and turned around. "Man, I can't believe I almost forgot. There's one more important thing."

Erin looked on the verge of tears, so Tess asked, "What is it?"

"You've met Eleanor, right?" Tom kept his voice low as he glanced back toward the kitchen.

"Yes."

"She has a granddaughter named Roshanna," Tom said. "Pastor Yazzi just talked to me about the family. Eleanor has convinced Roshanna to try VBS this year. She's never agreed to come before because she's been too afraid. So I'm putting you on the job to look out for her, to help her."

Tess took a step back. "Me?"

"Yes. You love kids, right? Roshanna told her grandmother she's always wanted a big sister. Well, this week that's you. I trust you. Don't let me down, okay?"

Tess tried to ignore her anxious heart. "Okay."

six

At the River

Sunday Evening, August 3; Monday, August 4

Tom left the table, and Tess and Erin quietly lined up to get dinner. After being served and praying, they sat down together.

"Tess, I just don't think I can do this. You know I'd do anything for my brother, and I wish I could help with kids, but I can't. I'm bad with them. They don't like me. They don't listen to me. I'll end up making a bigger mess for him than if I didn't help." Erin took a bite and swallowed before continuing. "I think you should ask Melissa to help you." Her eyes looked sad. "She would be a better choice. If you tell my brother, he'll agree."

Melissa did say she wished she were teaching, Tess thought. She looked at her friend and wondered how she could give Erin courage. "You can do it. I know you had a couple of bad experiences with little kids, but that was a long time ago. Besides, I want to do this with you. We're sisters, right? You and me. Like always." Tess ate a bite of her crispy fry bread.

Erin said nothing. Tess's voice softened. "If you don't

want to teach, then I'll ask Tom to have Melissa and Terri do it instead of you and me. But whatever we do, we do together, okay?"

"Okay," Erin said. "I'll think about it, and we can decide before we meet with Tom."

A few minutes later the two girls finished their meal and threw away their paper plates.

"I have to go to the bathroom, do you?" Erin asked.

"No, but I'll wait for you."

The two girls walked down the hallway, and while Erin went into the ladies' room, Tess stood outside the door. The room just to the right of the bathroom was another Sunday-school room.

Tess could overhear smooth Shannon and her friend talking. "We're all set for tomorrow. I have everything assembled on our tables downstairs, and I wrote the kids' names on some nametags," Shannon's friend said.

"Did you hear what Tom said about the new teachers?" Shannon asked.

Erin came out of the bathroom and was about to speak when Tess put her finger to her lips. "Shh."

Erin stood near Tess, and they listened together.

"Why does that Tess girl get to teach? She's not even a seventh-grader yet. It's only supposed to be older kids. She should do her time with kitchen duty first, like the rest of us," Shannon said.

"Isn't she the one on the bus who said Paul was one of the original disciples?" Shannon's friend asked. "I mean, no offense, but what if she teaches them something wrong?"

"And messes it up for the kids."

Tess opened her eyes wide. It was true. What if she did teach them something wrong?

"The only reason Erin is doing it is because her brother is in charge."

Erin stared at Tess and then motioned for Tess to keep walking down the hall before Shannon and her pal came out of the room. Erin and Tess quickly walked down to the sanctuary.

"So what do you think of that?" Tess asked.

"Tom did ask me because he's my brother," Erin said.

"No, he asked you because he knew you would be good," Tess said. "But—but what if I do make a mistake?"

"So what? Everybody does," Erin said. "We'll have the lesson plans."

Tess swallowed. "So do we do it?"

"It'll be really hard," Erin said. "I'm kind of afraid."

Tess recalled the words she had used last night when talking with Tom and repeated them now for Erin. "You never seemed like the kind of person who was afraid to try something hard."

Erin smiled. "You're right. And besides, Shannon is way wrong. We can do a good job." She looked a little nervous. "Can't we?"

Tess nodded. "We can."

Tom walked into the sanctuary. "Hi, guys. Thanks for helping me out. Let me tell you what to do." He handed them the teacher's notebooks as Tess and Erin sat up straight, determined to make things go right.

The Secret Sisters were up late Sunday night going over the lesson and then rose early Monday morning to make sure the VBS room was ready for the kids. Pastor Yazzi and Pastor Jack drove the big bus around the rural reservation, picking up kids near and far and bringing them to the church.

Some of the kids lived close by, though, including Roshanna. Tess kept watch for her, and soon Tess saw Eleanor walk up to the church, with a young girl and a baby lamb tagging alongside her. Roshanna stopped short of the church and clung to her grandmother's red skirt, not budging another step.

Now or never. Tess stepped out the front door and walked down the dirt path. When she stood in front of the girl, Tess knelt down.

"My name is Tess," she said. She pointed to the beaded barrettes in Roshanna's hair. "I wish I had some barrettes like that. They're so pretty."

Roshanna looked up and smiled but said nothing. From behind her, the little sheep bleated a scared cry.

"Is that your lamb?" Tess asked.

Roshanna nodded.

"I know a little song about a lamb. It goes, 'Mary had a little lamb, its fleece was white as snow, and everywhere that Mary went the lamb was sure to go. It followed her to school one day…'"

Roshanna giggled.

"Your lamb is following you to school, too, isn't it?" Tess teased. "We'll have to call you Mary." She held out her hand, and Roshanna took it.

"Can my lamb stay with me?"

Tess bit her lip. Oh, boy. She had figured out a lot of problems but not sheep problems.

"How about if we leave her tied up to the fence?" Tess

asked. "That way, you can look out the window and still see her."

Roshanna nodded, and Eleanor grinned. "I'll go home now. You walk home when you're done," she said to Roshanna.

Tess and Roshanna walked into the classroom together and sat down at the table that Tess and Erin were in charge of. Tess told the story of Joseph and his coat of many colors. She held up a picture.

"Hey," a happy little boy named Ben shouted out, "that looks like one of my mom's rugs!"

"You're right," Tess said. "It has many colors, like Navajo rugs."

While Erin nervously sat down in one of the kiddy chairs next to Angela, a little girl who never lifted her head, Tess read the story aloud of how Joseph was taken from his family. God used even a difficult time to work out what was best for Joseph and God's people. "God also gave some special friends to Joseph so he wouldn't feel lonely," she finished.

Roshanna looked at Tess and smiled.

Afterward, Erin passed out a picture of Joseph, some glue bottles, and many strings of yarn. The kids began to glue the yarn onto Joseph's coat. Roshanna never said a word through the whole morning, not to Tess nor to any of the other kids. Angela only lifted her head when Erin helped her with the craft.

After VBS, when the kids were leaving, Tess said, "Do you want me to walk you home, Roshanna?"

"No thank you," she said. "I go with my lamb." She walked out of the classroom, and Erin and Tess gave each other a high-five and then fell on the floor.

"We did it!" Tess said. She noticed a look of triumph in Erin's eyes.

"I'm wiped out! I never thought it would take that much energy! When's lunch?"

Tess smiled. She knew her friend felt better than she had the night before.

That night, while the rest of the group played some games, Pastor Jack rounded up Tess, Melissa, and the two boys who were to be baptized.

"We're going with Pastor Yazzi and the others while they dam up the river," Pastor Jack explained. "That way the water will be deep enough by Saturday for baptizing you guys. I'll send one of the older boys back tomorrow to make sure the water is damming well so that it'll be deep enough."

Tess slipped on her sandals and walked behind the others. The boys carried two big pieces of worn wood; Tess carried nails and a hammer; and Melissa carried four pieces of paper and a marker.

As they reached the rocky riverbed, Jack called them aside while Pastor Yazzi and several Navajo men began to partially dam the muddy river with rocks.

"I'll bet you're wondering what we're going to do with this wood," Pastor Jack started.

"Build a cross?" Melissa asked.

"Good guess," Jack said. "And you're right. We're making it public. That's what baptism is all about, making a public statement that you're a Christian, that you're living for Christ no matter what the cost."

A public statement. No matter the cost. Tess grew cool from the inside out.

Melissa and Tess held the wood while the boys nailed the pieces together. They propped up the cross in some rocks along the shore and then stood back. Late clouds crept across the sky, and the setting sun seemed to engulf the orange Shiprock Mountain.

"Now I want you each to write your name on a piece of paper."

Tess neatly wrote on her paper with the marker.

"And we're going to nail these papers to the cross. The Bible says we were crucified with Christ, and before we can rise again with him, symbolically through baptism, we need to spend a few days thinking about what dying with him means," Pastor Jack said. "Each of you take some time at the cross and tack up your names, then come and meet me at the top of that hill." He pointed some distance away. "I'm going to talk with Pastor Yazzi."

First Melissa tacked on her name while the others stood nearby. As she walked away, the others went forward and tacked on their names, then went to meet up with Pastor Jack. That left Tess.

She held on to her paper. It flapped in the gentle wind, but she didn't tack up her name. "What should I do, God?" she whispered into the wind. She heard nothing.

Looking around, Tess made sure nobody was watching her. Instead of tacking the paper onto the cross, she secretly folded up the sheet and slipped it into her pocket.

Tess wandered to the river alone, letting the chilly waves lap over her toes. Was she just going to dip her toes in the water, or was she going in all the way, no matter the cost?

seven

Cloudy

Tuesday, August 5

The next morning Tess and Erin set up all the materials for their Vacation Bible School table, excited to see what the kids would learn that day. Then the Secret Sisters waited at the door with the others; in a few minutes the VBS bus full of kids would arrive. The night before, the two of them had prayed for each of the kids, and Tess had prayed especially long for Roshanna while Erin prayed for Angela, the little girl who rarely lifted her head.

"We have service projects this afternoon," Erin said. "Do you want to sign up to help stack firewood or to sort through donated clothes in the thriftshop?"

"No way do I want to stack firewood," Tess said. "Gross. Probably has spiders. Let's work at the thriftshop. It'll be fun, like playing store."

"Cool," Erin agreed. "We'll go right after lunch."

Just then the bus pulled up, and a herd of kids tumbled out. The first few kids off laughed and teased each other, but others walked silently into the church.

"I'd better go to our table," Erin said.

Tess nodded. "I'll wait for Roshanna; then we'll come over."

As Erin walked to the small table where their little group of kids sat, Tess stood by the door, looking out over the warming morning, searching in the direction of Roshanna's house. Tess saw a great expanse of orange sand with a chunky brown mountain in the distance, but she didn't see Roshanna or her little lamb.

At ten minutes past the hour, Tess's worry about Roshanna grew stronger, but she decided she had better go to help Erin, who was about to read a story, and she looked really nervous. Tess glanced over at Shannon's table. All the kids sat perfectly still in their chairs, and Shannon looked in charge.

As Tess sat down beside Erin, Tom walked over to see how things were going. He scanned their group. "Where's Roshanna?"

Tess's heart raced. "I don't know. She didn't come this morning."

Tom's brows crinkled. "I thought you said everything went okay with her. I thought you said things seemed fine yesterday."

"They did seem fine!" Tess gulped air. "I mean, she seemed okay. She didn't cry or anything."

"Well, we told Pastor Yazzi we would take special care of her, and this isn't a good start." He looked at his watch.

The first big assignment Tom had given Tess, and she had messed it up. But how? The question wasn't really how, but how to fix it. "I could go and find her," Tess offered.

Tom looked up, a hopeful light in his eye. "Could you? I know her house. It's up the street a little, just over there,"

Tom pointed out the window toward a faded manufactured home. "See?"

"I could try."

"Do you feel okay about that?" Tom asked.

I don't want to mess this up for anyone. "Yes," Tess answered, although she wasn't thrilled to walk around a strange neighborhood in a place where she had been for only two days.

"All right."

"I'll be right back," she whispered in Erin's ear.

"What?" Erin said loudly. Even Angela looked up, but she looked scared.

"I'll be right back. Tell you more later." Tess slipped away before Erin could say any more. *Please, Lord, help her do okay.*

Tess stepped out the church door and walked down the dirt path toward Roshanna's house. The streets on the Navajo reservation had no names. Which house was Roshanna's? Two were together. She glanced back at the church behind her, as it grew smaller, and she felt like she was growing smaller, too, as she paced along.

She stopped at the small manufactured house at the end of a long drive. A little dog nipped at her hiking boots as she walked toward the door. She timidly knocked, just loud enough to be heard.

"Who is it?" A voice came from within. Relief flooded Tess's heart. Eleanor.

"It's me, Tess, from the Vacation Bible School," she called out.

"Oh, Tess, come on in."

Tess pushed open the door and walked into the small living area. Eleanor sat on the floor in front of a large, wooden loom. Strung across the thin, white strands of the loom was a nearly completed rug.

"I'm sorry I didn't get up," Eleanor said. "Old bones, you know. Arthritis. It's hard for me to stand up once I'm sitting."

"Oh, it's not a problem." Tess liked Eleanor, but Tess remained close to the door. She was in a stranger's house, and her parents wouldn't approve of her being there alone.

Eleanor said nothing, just sat weaving, threading yarn through the strings, then pushing it down with a wooden paddle.

Someone has to say something! Doesn't Eleanor care? "I came to see if Roshanna is okay. I—I missed her this morning at VBS."

Eleanor said nothing for a minute, concentrating on the yarn in front of her. "She was lonely for me. She's not used to church, you know. Her parents don't go, so she felt uncomfortable."

Believe me, I understand that, Tess thought. "Would it be okay if I talked with her?"

"Sure." Eleanor grabbed another ball of yarn from the shallow wooden bowl in front of her and pulled out some yarn. Then she wove it between the strings, never looking up at Tess while she did.

Why is she moving so slowly? Doesn't she want Roshanna to come? You would think she would be excited I was here to take Roshanna. Instead, Eleanor just kept weaving.

"Uh, well, where is she then?" Tess finally asked.

"She's out tending to the sheep. She'll be back in a few minutes. You can wait if you want."

Tess clasped her hands. She would wait five minutes.

Then she would have to go. It wasn't a good idea to wait here more than that, especially with Erin all alone. But Tess didn't want to let Tom down, so she waited.

"I hear you're going to have a baptism this weekend," Eleanor said. "My nephew helped to carry stones out to dam the river last night."

Tess unclasped her hands and stuck them in her pocket. The paper with her name on it was still there. Her secret. She held on to it while she spoke. "Yes, on Saturday." Eleanor said nothing. "I—I might be baptized."

Eleanor, her hands suddenly still, looked up at Tess. "Wonderful! I remember my baptism. One of the old men from the church came up and told me I'd never look more beautiful than I did that day. I think he was right." Her old eyes glazed over, remembering.

"Did your family come when you were baptized?" Tess asked, small beads of sweat breaking out on her forehead. *Please don't ask why I'm asking that.*

Eleanor shook her head. "My grandfather was a medicine man, and he thought when I took Christ I was rejecting the Navajo way. So he forbade anyone else from coming."

Eleanor smiled at Tess. "I'll come on Saturday. I like to celebrate." She chuckled for a minute, then took up her weaving.

Tess held her breath and let go of the paper in her pocket. She was about ready to leave when Roshanna burst in through the door.

"Help, *Shimashani,*" she said. Tess assumed that was the Navajo word for *grandmother.* "Help!"

"What happened?" Eleanor asked.

"Cloudy got her leg stuck in a snake hole, and I can't lift her out. I'm afraid she'll break her leg, and she's crying something awful. Her mommy is crying, too!"

"Cloudy?" Tess asked.

"Her lamb," Eleanor said. She tried to lumber to her feet but sank back down. "Ugh. Old bones. Useless."

"Don't get up," Tess said. "I can help." *At least I hope I can. But I know nothing about animals. What if I actually make things worse? Besides*—Tess looked at her watch—*Erin's probably flipping out that I've been gone so long.*

Eleanor stayed seated, and Roshanna looked so helpless that Tess knew she would have to try to help the little girl. No matter what.

"Thank you." Roshanna's sweaty little hand grabbed Tess's hand and pulled her toward the door.

eight

Erin's Troubles

Tuesday, August 5

Tess and Roshanna rushed out into the yard toward the back of the hogan where the sheep were penned. Even before Tess reached Cloudy, she could hear the baby's soft bleating and the mother's high, loud bleating.

"She's over here!" Roshanna dragged Tess to the back of the pen.

Tess looked into the baby lamb's hurting eyes. The mother sheep tried to butt into Tess.

"No!" Roshanna held back the mother sheep.

"Here, Cloudy, I can help." Tess knelt before the sheep as the baby bleated pitifully in her ear. She tried to lift out the leg, but it was locked into the hole.

"Please," Roshanna pleaded.

Tess scooted around to Cloudy's other side and bent the lamb's leg just a little. Finally, she gently lifted the sheep's foreleg, turning it as she did. Dusty sweat trickled from her forehead into her eyes. She grunted then lifted the entire baby lamb away from the hole.

"Cloudy!" Roshanna ran over and hugged the lamb,

putting her face deep into the soft wool. The lamb shook for a minute but then bleated happily and rubbed up next to Roshanna.

"We need to take her to my grandma. She can wrap up the leg." Roshanna touched just above the scraped skin on Cloudy's leg. "Thank you, Tess." Roshanna hugged her as Tess wiped the dirt off her knees. "But why are you at my house?"

"I missed you at Vacation Bible School," Tess said. "I waited for you at the door, but you didn't come. So I came to find you."

Roshanna hung her head. "I felt lonely and scared."

"Your grandmother goes to church," Tess offered.

"She wasn't there yesterday," Roshanna said. "No one in my family except Shimashani is a Christian. She wanted my brothers to go to VBS, but they wanted to play basketball with their friends. So I was all alone."

Tess sat there, letting the morning wind's warm breath blow through her hair. The stark landscape of orange sand and blue sky made the morning seem unhurried and peaceful. "How about if I'm like your family this week?" she asked.

"Like a big sister?" Roshanna's eyes lit up. "I've always wanted a big sister."

Tess nodded. "Like a big sister. I'm good at pretending to be sisters with people." She checked her watch again, thinking of her real Secret Sister.

Roshanna looked at Cloudy. "Can Cloudy come? And wait outside?"

"Yes, of course, 'Mary.'"

Roshanna remembered. "Mary had a little lamb, too, right?"

"Right." Tess smiled. "I'll see you tomorrow then?"

"Yes." Roshanna looked at her. "I promise, Big Sister." Then she giggled and walked back with her sheep while Tess hurried across the dusty yard and back onto the rutted dirt road that led to the church.

Hooray, I did it! Tom would be really proud of her, she was sure. She could barely wait to tell him, and she quickly arrived at the bright pink church.

Before she could even open the door, Tom burst out. "Tess, you're back!"

Tess stopped. "Of course."

Relief crossed his face. "I should never have sent you alone to a stranger's house. I just didn't want to look dumb in front of Pastor Jack or Pastor Yazzi. I'm sorry."

"It's okay. I—I did feel a little uncomfortable, but it all worked out."

"Okay. We had better get back inside. Erin needs your help."

Tess glanced over at their table. Erin glared at Tess and then glanced at the sobbing Angela.

"I'm sorry," Tess whispered. She drew near to her friend.

"Me, too!" Erin snapped back. "I told you I always make them cry! You go talk with Angela."

"No, you do it. I'm the one who needs to lead the crafts, remember?"

Erin nodded curtly and sat in a small chair next to Angela, whispering softly to her. Tess opened up the day's craft plan, passing out the materials.

God, she prayed silently, *I was in such a hurry not to let Tom down, but did I let Erin down instead?*

After a while Angela quit crying, and they finished the

day's lesson. Angela didn't cry again but didn't smile either as Erin put her on the bus.

"Erin," Tess began, "I'm sorry. Angela wasn't crying yesterday."

"That's because I wasn't in charge yesterday!" Erin snapped.

"That's not true. I mean—"

"Tess, please let's not talk about it now. I'm tired."

"I talked with Roshanna. She'll be back tomorrow," Tess said.

"I'll bet Angela won't," Erin answered. "You got one back, and I scared one away."

Tess was about to say something encouraging to Erin when Erin began to walk toward the lunchroom. "Let's eat. Then we have to get to the thrift store."

Tess followed but said nothing.

Later that afternoon Erin perked up a little as they looked around the thriftshop's back room. "I've never seen such a mess in my whole life." Erin giggled. "Not even your room looks this bad."

"Ha-ha," Tess said, glad to see her friend joking. She looked around. At least a hundred plastic garbage bags stuffed with clothes, pots and pans, and faded toys stood stacked all around them. Some of the bags were ripped, their insides spilling out like fabric guts all over the floor.

"What are we supposed to do?" Erin asked.

"You signed us up for this service project, you find out," Tess kidded.

As Erin rolled her eyes and began to leave the room to

find one of the Navajo women, Tess called out, "Hey, I forgot to tell you something."

Erin turned around.

"Since you signed us up for this project, I signed us up for one on Thursday."

"Which one?"

"Painting."

"Oh no, not painting. Remember when we painted my grandparents' fence? How we were covered with paint?"

"Oh yes, I remember." Tess laughed. "And I have a surprise for you."

"What is it?"

"I said it was a surprise. You have to wait till Thursday."

Erin picked up a clean shirt from the floor and tossed it at Tess. "Thanks a lot." The shirt landed on Tess's head, and Erin went to ask a supervisor what they were supposed to do.

After several hours of unloading bags and folding clothes, Erin stacked the clothes on shelves, and Tess went to clean out the try-on rooms. In one of them she found a netted lady's hat and a large, floral-print dress. She pulled it on over her clothes and went to show Erin, who still was sorting in the back room.

Tess giggled. "I'm thinking of wearing this to dinner, what do you think?"

"Only if I can wear this." Erin flopped a ratty wig on her head.

"You look like a commercial for the Manly Hair Club." Tess laughed. "I'd better get back to the try-on rooms." She took off her costume and then finished cleaning up before rejoining Erin, who was still stacking clothes.

"So how was the baptism thing at the river yesterday?" Erin asked. "We were so worried last night about planning today's lesson I forgot to ask you. I'm glad your parents took the news okay."

"What news?" Tess stopped stacking.

"About your being baptized. That they said yes."

Tess sat on the floor. "Erin, I haven't told them yet."

"*What?* You know Pastor Jack won't baptize you without their permission!" Erin sat down next to her.

"I know. And I wouldn't want to do it without their permission. It's just that a lot of things were going on, and it wasn't the right time to tell them." She didn't want to add to Erin's troubles by telling her that Tess's parents weren't too cool about driving Tess to church, which was why she couldn't mention baptism to them.

"What are you going to do?" Erin asked.

"I guess I need to answer the baptism questions. And pray. Make sure God wants me to get baptized now. I mean, maybe he wants me to wait." Tess's hands shook as she grabbed the last stack of clothes. "I need to figure it all out before I rock my parents' boat, you know?" Even thinking about talking to her parents about baptism brought fear to her skin's surface.

"Yeah, we can pray together."

Tess was about to mention the piece of paper in her pocket with her name on it and how she hadn't tacked it to the cross, but Erin's gaze shifted toward the door. A small Navajo girl and her mother walked into the thriftshop.

"She looks like Angela, doesn't she?" Erin asked.

"Yes," Tess agreed.

"I hope Angela comes tomorrow," Erin said in a small voice.

nine

A Private Talk

Wednesday, August 6

The next morning, Tess and Erin got up early and prayed—
prayed that Roshanna would come, prayed that Angela
would come, and prayed that Tess would know what to do
about being baptized. Then they walked downstairs and
waited to see how their prayers would be answered.

The busload of VBS kids already had arrived, and the
kids were settling in. Chubby-cheeked Ben sat happily at
their table playing with an action figure that the boy next
to him was very interested in. Finally Angela arrived, cling-
ing to her mother's hand. Erin's grin electrified the room.

"She was afraid, but she didn't want Teacher Erin to be
sad," Angela's mother commented as she brought Angela
over to the table. "Which one of you is Erin?"

Erin introduced herself.

"Angela tells me you like horses. So do we." Angela's
mother smiled as she left.

Angela said nothing but sat down in the seat closest to
Erin.

Tess looked out the front door. Roshanna was nowhere in

sight. Tess looked to the far corner of the room. Shannon's group, of course, was all there. Tess closed her eyes. *Please, God, let her come.*

A few minutes later a bleating sounded down the street. A warm smile spread across Tess's face. Cloudy.

"Hi, Big Sister!" Roshanna called out, waving at Tess and revealing a missing tooth as she smiled.

Tess realized it was the first time she had seen Roshanna smile. "Hi!" Tess called back as she practically skipped out front. "Let's tie Cloudy to the fence so she doesn't wander away. Then we had better get inside and join the rest of the kids at our table." They secured Cloudy and walked hand-in-hand into the VBS room.

Roshanna headed toward the table but seemed reluctant to sit down. Just as Roshanna was turning toward Tess, Angela spoke for the first time. "Sit here." She patted the empty seat beside her. Then she scooted her own chair over to make room for Roshanna to squeeze in.

Tess smiled at Erin, and Erin smiled back and began to read the story. "Today, we're going to learn about Joshua and the wall of Jericho."

When Erin finished the story, she said, "The Lord told the people he would be with them when they were doing hard things. In fact, even though he expected them to obey him, he would do all the work. The Israelites' job was to obey God; God would do the rest."

Obey me, came a whisper inside Tess's heart. The voice seemed so strong she nearly dropped her Bible.

I'm trying! she responded.

"Okay!" Tess clapped her hands. "Who's ready to build a wall?"

"Me, me, me!" shouted the little voices. Tess and Erin

pushed their table aside and brought out a big box of blocks. Erin knelt while the kids built an enormous wall of blocks around her.

Tess helped build, too, keeping her eye on Roshanna, who happily talked with her new friend Angela. Roshanna came over to hold hands with Tess only once. And Angela giggled every now and then.

As soon as the wall completely hid Erin, Tess opened a box loaned to them by Pastor Yazzi. She reached inside and pulled out something. "Who knows what this is?"

"A sheep's horn!" Ben yelled out. *Of course they would know.* Tess smiled. *They have sheep all over the place here!*

She passed a horn to each of the kids, and they pretended to blow on it as they marched around the wall. The seventh time around they all shouted as loud as they could, and Erin, from inside the wall, knocked down all the blocks.

The kids fell into the blocks, laughing.

"Can we build another wall?" Roshanna asked.

"Sure," Tess said. They began to build the wall again, ready to have more fun.

After the kids had gone home, Erin beamed. "I think we did it! I think we're a success!"

"Well," Tess answered, "you are. Angela loves you. And Angela and Roshanna had a great time."

"What do you mean, *I* am?" Erin looked puzzled. "You're a success, too."

"Yeah, but you were worried about being with the kids. You did it. My big worry is not making a mistake in what I teach them, remember? The gospel lesson comes Friday. I've never done it before. I don't want to prove Shannon right about me; I don't want to fail Tom, and I *really* don't want to mess up the story for these kids."

"So?" Erin said.

"Listen." Tess pulled back her hair from her neck and fanned herself. "I think you should teach it. I have a lot on my mind. You know, baptism and all."

"You're just worried about messing up."

Tess nodded.

"You can do it." Erin began to put away the crafts.

Tess turned so Erin wouldn't see her cheeks flush with anger. *Easy for you to say. You've been a Christian all your life.*

"Let's eat lunch at the flea market," Erin said after they had cleaned up their area. "Everyone else is going."

"Oh, all right," Tess agreed with a sigh. Friday's lesson was two days away.

They set out walking. Less than a mile later they reached the collection of weathered plywood building barely held together with rusty nails. Some of the stalls at the flea market were simply card tables with traditional crafts for sale. Thick blankets sheltered some of the valuables, keeping off the dust. The scent of hot oil slithered through the air—fry bread was cooking nearby.

"Let's shop first." Erin wandered over to a table that had small Navajo rugs. Tess gingerly touched the scratchy wool of a beautiful red and brown rug.

Erin pulled her wallet out of her pocket. "My mom gave me money to buy a rug." She felt each rug and finally chose one with turquoise blue and sea green.

Tess patted her wallet. *I have to save enough to give to Pastor Jack to buy the surprises when he goes to town tonight.*

Tess walked to another table and purchased a matching pair of beaded barrettes. "For my best friend and me," she told the Navajo grandmother behind the table. Then Tess bought a beaded baby doll for Tara and a pack of feathers for Tyler and tucked them all in her backpack.

"Ready to eat?" Erin came up alongside her.

"Starving." They walked to one of the buildings with a door on it. A handwritten menu was tacked to the door. "Should we go in?" Tess asked.

"I guess so. I hope it's okay." Erin opened the door, and ten sets of Navajo eyes were on the girls, the only non-Indians in the room. After a minute, the conversation resumed. The girls sat down and waited.

"Does someone come to take our order?" Erin swatted away a persistent fly.

"I don't know."

As Tess answered, a young man approached their picnic table, smiling. "Can I help you?"

Tess read the simple menu written by hand and taped to one wall. "I'd like some fry bread and some vegetable stew. And a can of pop."

"Me, too." Erin didn't even look at the menu.

"All right, just a few minutes," the man assured them before leaving.

"Did I really do okay today?" Erin asked.

"You heard Angela's mom," Tess said. "And I'm so glad for Roshanna and Angela. Everything is better when you have a friend."

"You're my best friend." Erin smiled across the table at Tess. "I could never have done this without my Secret Sister."

"You did great," Tess said. "In fact, I don't think I'll have time to baby-sit for both the Kims and the Fyes this fall. Why don't I recommend you to Mrs. Kim?"

"Really?" Erin asked.

"Really."

Their food arrived, and they ate up the delicious stew and bread.

Halfway through her bowl of stew, Tess looked up as the crooked door to the little shack opened. Tom walked in. He aimed straight for Tess, but he wasn't smiling.

"I think we should talk when you're done," he said to her. "In private."

ten

Handprints

Wednesday, August 6; Thursday, August 7

"Um, okay." Tess left her bowl at the table and followed Tom to another table.

"Listen." He stared at her across the rough planks of the picnic table. "What's up with the baptism? Your name isn't on the cross."

The vegetable stew began to churn in Tess's stomach. "How did you know?"

"I went out to check the water level. I stopped by and looked at the cross and saw the other three had their names up, but not you. I was wondering what happened. Pastor Jack will wonder the same thing if he goes out there before tomorrow."

"I want to make sure I'm doing the right thing. I—I'm still working on the baptism questions, and then I'll talk with Pastor Jack." Tess tapped her fingers against the table. "I want to make sure I'm doing it for the right reasons. I've been so busy preparing for VBS, I haven't even had time to finish my baptism questions. I wasn't going to nail my name to the cross and then take it down." She swallowed.

"I haven't asked my parents yet."

"Oh." Tom's face softened. "I see. That's pretty rough."
He smiled at her. "I won't say anything to Pastor Jack,
but if he goes down to the river before you talk with him,
he's going to see the cross. Without your name on it."

"I know," Tess said. "I'll deal with that if it happens."

"I'll keep your secret," Tom said. "And pray for you.
Thanks for the great work you're doing with the kids."

"No problem." Tess grinned at him. "You can eat with
us, if you want." They walked back to the table where Erin
sat waiting.

Erin looked at Tess as if to say, "What's up?"

"I'll tell you later," Tess whispered into Erin's ear as Tom
ordered his lunch.

The three of them joked while Tom finished eating, then
Tess and Erin headed back to their room.

"What was that all about?" Erin asked.

Tess sat down on her rolled-up sleeping bag. "Remember at the thrift store when I told you I wasn't sure about
baptism?"

"Yeah."

"Well, I didn't finish the story because we changed the
subject." Tess closed the door and sat back down. "Do you
remember the day those of us who are getting baptized
went to dam up the river?"

Erin nodded.

"Well, we each were given a piece of paper and wrote
our names on them. Pastor Jack told us to tack our names
to the cross before we were baptized." Tess reached into
her pocket and withdrew the piece of paper with her name
on it. "Here's mine. Tom saw that mine wasn't on the cross,
and he confronted me."

"Oh no! What are you going to do?"

"Tom won't say anything to Pastor Jack until I meet with him tomorrow. Maybe Pastor Jack will say I'm not ready. I mean, maybe I'm not. And then I could be baptized with you guys. You know, give my parents time to prepare."

"What if Pastor Jack says you are ready?"

Tess gulped. "I don't know."

Erin nodded sympathetically and stood up. "I'm glad you told me. We had better go work on the service project for today. Cleaning the shed."

The next afternoon Tess and Erin dragged cans of paint from the newly cleaned shed out to the church's storage building. Tess kicked away a small spider crawling across the dirt floor. "Guess we knocked her web down yesterday."

The VBS team and the Navajo kids worked to put a fresh, pink coat of paint over the church's storage building, which had grown chipped from dusty wind and cold. Tom had a ladder that reached the top. Some of the littlest Navajo kids painted the bottom; sometimes their brushes scraped into the dirt, and Tess or another girl would wash them off.

Eleanor came out of the kitchen where she had made their lunches. "I'd like you to be my family's guest at dinner tonight," she said to Tess, who was painting a corner of the building. "Your friend, too." Eleanor pointed to Erin. "You've been a big help to Roshanna. She's having fun at church."

"I'll ask Pastor Jack. If he says okay, I'd love to come,"

Tess said. Erin nodded her agreement, and Eleanor smiled, wiped her hands on her apron, and walked back into the kitchen.

A few minutes later, Pastor Yazzi stood in front of the freshly painted building. "Tess had a good idea," he said. "She asked Jack, who told me about it a couple of days ago. Do you want to tell everyone, Tess?"

Tess's eyes opened wide. She hadn't realized he was going to have her make the announcement. "Well, I got the idea from Eleanor, Roshanna's grandma," Tess said. Roshanna beamed.

"Our first night here Eleanor said something about helping hands, so I thought maybe we could paint our hands in blue or white and then each put our handprint at the bottom of the back wall. Then we'll have a place to show that we all worked together, Living Water kids and Navajo kids. Hand in hand."

"Great idea," Tom called out. Shannon kept cleaning her paintbrush, never looking at Tess. Tess stared at her back. She hoped Shannon wouldn't be listening when she shared the gospel with the kids on Friday.

One by one, the kids painted their hands and put their handprints on the wall. First a big kid would make a set of handprints, then a little kid, then another big kid, until almost everyone had made a mark on the building.

"Look! Our fingertips touch!" Roshanna giggled as she and Angela, the last two little kids to paint their hands, put their handprints together.

"Yeah, like we're sisters." Angela giggled back.

Tess and Erin looked at each other. They must have had the same idea at the same time. "Hey," Tess said, "that gives me a fabulous idea." She leaned and whispered in Erin's ear, and Erin nodded enthusiastically before the two of them sat on the ground with Roshanna and Angela.

"Erin and I are Secret Sisters," Tess explained. "It's like we're best friends but even more special. Sisters. We help each other with everything, even the hard stuff, and we stick together no matter what."

"Just like us!" Roshanna grabbed Angela's hand.

"Exactly," Erin said. "Why don't you guys be Secret Sisters, too? Then, after Tess and I go home, you'll always have each other."

Angela giggled and nodded yes. Roshanna just beamed.

"We'll be the big Secret Sisters, and you'll be the little Secret Sisters," Tess said.

She and Erin put their handprints right above Angela and Roshanna's on the wall. "And now, I have another surprise," Tess said. She led the other Secret Sisters to a side table.

"This is why I saved some of my money yesterday," she said. Reaching inside a bag, she pulled out four T-shirts: two big ones and two little ones. "I asked Pastor Jack to buy these when he went into town yesterday." She spread them across the table. "I didn't know then that you guys were going to be little Secret Sisters, but now it's even more special. Watch." Tess painted her hands again, and put her handprints on the front of one of the big shirts, then painted her hands again and again until her prints were on all four shirts.

"Now you three do the same. Then we'll each have a shirt to remind us of working for the Lord, hand in hand, no matter if we're separated or not."

Erin smiled and walked over to the table to paint her hands. Then Tess painted Roshanna's hands while she laughed, and Erin painted Angela's.

"That tickles!" Angela giggled as the paintbrush crossed her palms.

The four of them set their shirts aside to dry and began to help the cleanup crew. For just a minute, Tess stood back and watched the laughter and fun. All around her, like a great swirl of warmth that made her head light, she felt God's presence, his pleasure at being in the midst of his people, as he said he would be.

This is church, Tess thought. *God is with us, and we are honoring him together. Although I'll miss Erin, I want to keep going to church.*

"Great idea about the handprints on the wall, Tess." Melissa walked up. "You always have great ideas. I hope you'll teach preschool with me this fall."

Tess smiled. Melissa hadn't said one rude word about Tess and Erin getting to teach at VBS while Melissa and Terri had to do kitchen crew, even though Tess knew Melissa wanted to teach. She was a good friend.

Tess had an idea. "I want to teach, but there's a problem."

"What is it?"

"Well," Tess began, "Erin's family has to go to another church for a few months, to help her grandpa. So I might not have a ride to church. I—I wondered, if my parents allow me to come, would you be willing to help with rides?"

"Sure!" Melissa rushed in. "I'll go ask my mom." She ran over to the side of the building where the adults were capping paint cans. A minute later she returned. "My mom said it would be fine. She'll even call your mom."

"Not yet!" Tess blurted out. "I mean, thanks, but I'll call you first. Okay?"

I don't even know if they'll say yes since they think I'm too involved. She glanced at Pastor Jack, who was talking with Paul and Jamie, the two boys who were to be baptized. *I have another conversation to tackle first.*

eleven

Two Hands

Thursday Night, August 7

Tess asked permission to go to Eleanor's for dinner, and Pastor Jack said that, yes, both Tess and Erin could go. A couple of hours later, while the others ate in the dining room, the Secret Sisters finished preparing to visit Eleanor's home.

"I'm kind of nervous. I don't know why." Tess smoothed her hands over a clean pair of jeans and tucked in her T-shirt. "I'm glad we're going together."

Within a couple of minutes they arrived at Eleanor's tidy home. Tess knocked on the door, and Eleanor answered.

"Come in, come in," she said. They stepped into the tiny living room where a man sat on the couch. He stood up when the girls came in.

"This is my daughter's husband, Joseph," Eleanor said. Joseph smiled warmly, nodded, and sat down again to watch an old movie on the TV.

A woman came out of the kitchen. "Hello," she said shyly. "I'm Gloria, Roshanna's mother." She wiped her hands on her apron.

"Nice to meet you," Tess said.

Roshanna raced into the room, holding hands with Angela. "Surprise!" the girls squealed, each wearing a Secret Sisters T-shirt.

"This *is* a surprise," Tess said.

"Roshanna told me what good friends they had become." Eleanor grinned. "I asked Angela's mother if she could come tonight, too."

"Dinner, dinner, dinner," Roshanna sang out. "I'm hungry, and my mom makes the best mutton stew."

As they walked to the table, Tess whispered to Erin, "What exactly is mutton?"

"I don't know," Erin whispered back. "But we have to eat it."

They sat at two card tables squeezed together, chairs of varying sizes arranged in even rows. Roshanna's brothers joined them, and Joseph sat at the head of the table.

As soon as the meal was served, they began to eat. About halfway through a piece of sweet, chewy fry bread, Tess took a bite of her mutton stew. Hmm, it was good. Roshanna was right. Tess ate up almost the whole bowl.

"This is delicious." Erin spooned up the last bit of broth.

"Thank you." Gloria smiled. An old sheep bleated in the background.

"There's next week's mutton stew," one of Roshanna's brothers joked. The rest of his family laughed as Tess nearly choked on her stew.

"Are you okay?" Eleanor asked.

"Oh, uh, I'm fine, thanks." She was eating lamb? Like baby Cloudy? Tess slowly pushed away her bowl, hoping no one would notice, and concentrated on the fry bread.

"Does your grandma make fry bread for dinner?" Roshanna asked.

"My grandma doesn't know how to make fry bread. And we don't eat dinner with her. We only see her a couple of times a year."

Roshanna's eyes opened wide. "Oh. I'm sorry, that must be sad for you." She turned toward Erin. "Do you live with your grandma?"

"No. But I'll see her every week this fall."

"Sad." Roshanna faced her bowl again. Angela shook her head in pity. Even Roshanna's brothers looked at Tess and Erin with compassion.

Funny, I felt sorry for them having to live in such a small, poor place. But they're feeling sorry for me!

"Can we be done, Mom?"

Roshanna's mother nodded, and Roshanna pushed her chair away from the table. The brothers left the room.

"Eleanor, could you please show me your loom?" Erin asked. "I bought a rug for my mother."

Eleanor beamed.

"I'll clean the dishes, Mom," Gloria said.

After thanking Roshanna's mother for the food, Tess, Erin, Angela, and Roshanna went to Eleanor's loom.

"It's called 'The Tree of Life,'" she said, as they all examined the beautiful rug she was working on. "Many stories tell what it means. Different weavers have different ideas. For me, it reminds me of the tree of life in Proverbs." She touched the delicate threads of brown and beige; colorful birds perched on the branches. "It's for Roshanna."

"So pretty," Erin said. "How do you do it?"

Erin sat down in front of the loom while Eleanor showed her how to weave a thread throughout.

"Would you like to try?"

"Sure." Erin wove part of one thread and then stood up.

"And now," Roshanna grabbed Tess's hand, "horseback riding!"

Tess and Erin looked at one another.

"That is, if you'd like to ride." Roshanna's dad stepped between them. "The horses are very gentle. We have two, and Angela's mother brought theirs."

"Yes, we'd love it!" Tess said. They walked outside and behind the house, where two of the horses already were saddled up for Tess and Erin.

"We'll ride bareback," Joseph said. "We're used to it."

All four girls patted and spoke softly to their horses before mounting them. Joseph mounted his horse, too.

Tess gently nudged the side of her paint pony, and it began to walk. The desert behind Roshanna's house was as endless and open as the ocean, with little ripples in the sand like water. The setting sun looked like a blood orange, and it sank behind mountains that grew dark brown as night fell. Tess breathed in the sage-perfumed air.

"I'm glad you came to our home," Roshanna said.

"I'm glad I came, too," Tess agreed.

"Angela and I will be Secret Sisters after you leave. Isn't that neat?"

Erin smiled at Tess before Tess answered. Tess patted her horse. "It *is* neat, Roshanna."

The twilight wind blew softly, lifting the horses' manes, as they walked gently back toward the house. Tess and Erin rode behind the others, bringing up the rear.

"It's beautiful out here, isn't it?" Erin said.

"Yes." The day was coming to an end, and anxious thoughts began to choke the peace in Tess's heart. "But tomorrow's Friday and the big lesson. The gospel."

Erin nodded and smiled encouragingly.

I don't want to mess it up, God, Tess said inside. *I have no clue what I'm doing here.*

They walked the horses to the fence and tied them up. In the deep purple night, Tess watched with affection as Roshanna and Angela giggled.

Help me to do it right for their sake.

twelve

Lost Sheep

Friday Morning, August 8

"Who needs more glue?' Erin walked around their table the next morning, squirting pools of glue onto the paper plates in front of the VBS kids.

Angela raised her hand. After Erin refilled Angela's glue, Angela picked up another cotton ball and stuck it onto her paper on which was drawn a lamb. The cotton balls made the soft wool.

"Can you write 'Cloudy' on my paper?" Roshanna tugged on Tess's sleeve.

Tess looked up from her lesson and scribbled the baby lamb's name on Roshanna's paper.

"Ready?" Erin whispered.

Tess looked over toward the other VBS groups, most of which already had started their stories. She spied Shannon, reading calmly to her group, not nervous at all.

Not like me.

"We're just like these sheep." Tess opened her Bible. "Let me read to you. Then Jesus told them this story: "Suppose one of you has 100 sheep, but he loses 1 of them.

Then he will leave the other 99 sheep alone and go out and look for the lost sheep."'"

Tess looked at the kids. Everyone watched her, but not even cheery Ben smiled.

She went back to reading. "'The man will keep on searching for the lost sheep until he finds it. And when he finds it, the man is very happy. He puts it on his shoulders and goes home. He calls to his friends and neighbors and says, "Be happy with me because I found my lost sheep!" In the same way, I tell you there is much joy in heaven when 1 sinner changes his heart.'"

"We lost a sheep once," Ben offered, his chubby cheeks wobbling as he spoke.

"What happened?" Tess asked.

"My mom went out with the dog and found it. I was so happy."

"Just like Jesus is when one of his lost sheep comes home." Tess looked at the kids. "Jesus wants to be your friend, your Savior. He wants to be with you, and he will, if you ask him into your heart. Do you understand?"

Each child nodded yes somberly.

"Would anyone like to ask Jesus into his heart, like we talked about before?"

Five stony faces looked back at her. Finally, Ben raised his hand. Tess smiled and drew him aside. She prayed with him, and after he returned to his seat, she wrote his name down on a special card Pastor Jack had given her to pass along to Pastor Yazzi.

But her joy was mixed with sorrow. Only one child. And, she was sorry to say, not Roshanna. Tess's heart sank. She must have said something wrong. But what? She had read the Bible. Maybe she should have explained more. But the rest of the kids in the room were packing up to go home, and their five were eager to go, too.

The whole VBS gathered together to sing a few last songs. As Tess looked over the crowd of kids, she felt a wave of sadness. She would never see these kids again. Would they remember her?

"Do you want to walk me home?" Roshanna asked.

"Sure." Tess told Erin, "I'm going to walk Roshanna home. Then I have to meet with Pastor Jack."

Erin squeezed Tess's hand. "I'll pray for you. Come and find me right away after you talk to Pastor Jack."

Tess nodded, and then she, Roshanna, and Cloudy set off toward Eleanor's house.

After a minute of silence, Roshanna said, "I didn't know Jesus had sheep in heaven."

Tess stopped walking and bent down to Roshanna's level. "What do you mean?"

"You said that Jesus is happy when one of his sheep comes home."

Tess took Roshanna's hand in her own. "Remember when I said we are like sheep? When the Bible says lost sheep, it means all the people who don't yet know about Jesus, who haven't trusted him to save them."

Roshanna's dark brown eyes looked back at Tess, her black bangs brushing against her eyebrows. "Am I a lost sheep?"

A sudden rush of excitement hit Tess's heart. "Yes, you are. But you don't have to stay lost. You can be safe at home with Jesus. Do you want to ask Jesus if you could please be one of his sheep?"

Roshanna stared back at her. "Will I have to go to church?"

For a minute Tess was tempted to tell her no, if only to get her to become a Christian. In the far corner of Tess's mind she could hear her dad saying, "You can read your Bible and pray at home." But she knew now that wasn't right.

"It's important to go; think of all you can learn there! Your grandma will be there with you, and you can ask Angela. Jesus will never leave you alone, not in church or anywhere."

Roshanna nodded. "I want to be a Christian." She clutched her cotton sheep paper in her hand. "What do I do?"

Tess kept hold of Roshanna's hand. "You pray, 'Jesus, I'm a lost sheep. I want to be warm and safe with you. I'm sorry for all the mistakes and bad choices I've made. Please forgive me. And help me to trust in you now. Amen.'"

Roshanna squeezed her eyes shut and prayed the words. Tess's heart filled with joy.

"Come on, let's race!" Roshanna said.

"I'm pretty fast!" Tess answered. The two of them tore down the road, kicking up a haze of dust behind them.

When they reached Eleanor's house, Roshanna went to put Cloudy in the back while Tess knocked on the front door.

"Come in," Eleanor called.

Tess burst into the house. Eleanor was on the floor, weaving.

"Guess what?"

Eleanor's kind face looked up.

"Roshanna asked Christ into her heart. Just a few minutes ago."

A slow smile spread across Eleanor's wrinkled face. "Hallelujah. I've felt for a long while that she was just about ready. Come here."

Tess knelt down beside her, and Eleanor hugged her. Then Eleanor handed Tess a piece of yarn. "Here, I'll show you."

Patiently, her hands over Tess's hands, Eleanor guided the thread through all the spider-web thin strings of the loom. Next Tess beat the thread into the rest of the rug with a wooden paddle.

"You've woven a thread of yourself into Roshanna's life," Eleanor said. "I wanted you to weave a thread into her Tree of Life rug. It will always be there, silently speaking of you."

Tess brushed away a tear. "This is one of the best days of my life." She hugged Eleanor and stood up. Then she glanced at her watch. "I—I'd better get going. I have to meet with Pastor Jack in a little bit."

"Okay." Eleanor didn't look up from her loom. "I'll see you at your baptism tomorrow."

Tess didn't answer.

thirteen

Time to Stand

Friday Afternoon, August 8

On the way back to the church, Tess passed the riverbank. She glanced at her watch. *I have a couple of minutes.* The sound of the river drew her, and she walked toward the water.

Once there, Tess kicked off her sandals. She let the cold water engulf her ankles and the sand squish between her toes. The rocks had dammed up a considerably deep area, ready for the baptism. She stared at the pool of water for a minute, then stepped back out of the river. *Jesus was baptized in a river,* she remembered with a smile. *Cool.*

A couple of feet away were rows of rocks, rocks she would sit on tomorrow as she watched the others be baptized. Choosing a smooth one, she sat down and stared for a minute at the wooden cross they had erected a few nights before. Then Tess pulled her baptism questionnaire out of her backpack.

"Baptism is a symbol," she read into the wind. "It symbolizes death and new life. Death to the old way of living, new life in Christ. Does that describe you?"

Underneath, she had checked, "Yes." She nodded her head in silence and scanned the next page.

"Who is it a symbol for? For the person being baptized, to remind her of her place in God's family, and as a public symbol to others that she has a new life in Christ."

She heard a noise behind her and turned around.

Tom.

He walked over and sat next to her. "I came to check to make sure the water was deep enough. I'm feeling better now that VBS is over and it went well."

"You did a great job."

"Thanks. I really appreciate all your help. What are you doing here?"

"I'm going to talk with Pastor Jack in a minute. I stopped here to think."

"What have you decided?"

Obey me came the whisper to her heart.

"I think I'm supposed to do it now, but I'm a little afraid to talk to Pastor Jack and more than a little afraid to tell my parents. I know that baptism is about being public about your faith, and I don't mind doing it in front of everyone. But I'm afraid about my parents."

Tom looked at her. "I never thought you were the kind of person who was afraid to try something hard." He smiled, and Tess, recognizing her own words coming back at her, smiled in return.

"Yeah, well," she said.

"I'll leave you alone," he said.

"Thanks."

As Tom walked back up the hill, Tess closed the baptism questionnaire and prepared to put it away. Out of the corner of her eye she caught a single verse on the back of the paper. "If anyone stands before other people and says he believes in me, then I will say that he belongs to me. I will say this before my Father in heaven (Matthew 10:32)."

It's time to stand.

Tess slipped the questionnaire into her backpack. As she did, her hand brushed against the slip of paper with her name on it. The night before she had taken it from her pocket and had tossed it into her pack. She felt in the front small pocket for the tacks she had stuffed in there when hanging papers on the VBS bulletin board. Then she walked to the cross.

In the wind, in front of God, she held the paper marked "Tess" in her hand and tacked it to the cross. Then she walked up the riverbank toward the church and hoped that everything that must follow would work out okay. There was no turning back now.

"I'm sorry I'm late," Tess said, as she walked into the church's sanctuary to meet with Pastor Jack. He sat in a pew about three rows back.

"Don't worry about it; it's just a few minutes," he answered.

"I have really good news!" *You're stalling your confession,* she thought to herself.

"Tell me!" Jack smiled.

"Well, this morning Ben accepted Jesus during VBS, and then, when I walked Roshanna home, she asked me how to become a Christian. So I told her, and she did. Isn't that cool?"

"Way cool," Pastor Jack agreed, grinning. "Peter Yazzi

will be thrilled. We had a couple of other kids make decisions, too. I'll make sure to tell Peter today so he can prepare the Sunday-school teachers. Did you tell Eleanor?"

Tess nodded. "She was happy, too."

Five long seconds ticked by before Pastor Jack asked the next question. "Did you bring your papers?"

Tess nodded. She handed the three pages, slightly wrinkled and stained with water drops, to Jack. He read over the questions and her answers.

As the minutes slipped by in slow motion, Tess's breathing grew faster. *Maybe he won't like my answers and will tell me to wait. I can't do it if he says wait, can I?*

Jack flipped over the pages and closed the booklet. "You're ready."

"I am?"

"You are. You've had quite a year, haven't you? Last summer you didn't know anything about Jesus, and now here you are ready to be baptized. Do you still want to be baptized?"

"Yes," Tess said. "I want to obey, and to, uh, stand up for Jesus in public. Doing it in a river, like Jesus did, is cool. But…"

Jack leaned in closer. "Worried about the river? It's perfectly safe."

"No, no, I'm not worried about the river. It's just that, well…" Tess took a deep breath. "I haven't asked my parents." She scooted back, as if fearing a blast of anger. But none came.

"Aha. This is a problem," Jack said. "Why didn't you tell them?"

Relieved that the truth was out, Tess explained to him

about her parents not wanting her to go to church when Erin left for a few months. That she was worried her dad would be angry. That her parents thought she was over-involved. And that she hadn't wanted to bring it up before she was really sure she should be baptized now.

"I understand. But you know I won't baptize you without your parents' permission."

Tess nodded.

"And I know you well enough that you wouldn't want to do it without their permission."

Tess nodded again.

"So that leaves calling them. You can use the phone at the church office," Pastor Jack said. "I'll walk you down there and introduce you to the secretary. They close up early, though, so you'll have to call soon. Will your parents be home?"

"I think so. My dad skips lunch so he can go home a little early and help with the baby."

"Then let's get to the office." They walked together down the narrow, dark hallway from the sanctuary to the office.

"Betty," Jack said to the secretary, "is there a private room where Tess can use the telephone?"

Betty smiled and led Tess to Pastor Yazzi's office. "I'm sure Peter won't mind."

"I'll wait for you in the sanctuary," Jack said. "Come on down after you call and let me know how it went. I'll be praying for you." Then he turned and left the office.

Tess walked into Pastor Yazzi's office and closed the door. She sat in his big chair for a minute, feeling like Goldilocks in Papa Bear's chair. And Papa Bear was about to get bad news.

She lifted the phone receiver and dialed the number to her house.

Maybe no one will answer.

She heard a click as someone on the other end lifted the receiver.

"Hello?"

fourteen

Dad

Friday, August 8

"Tyler, is that you?" Tess asked.

"Tess, is that you?" he echoed back.

"Yes, of course, goofy." She glanced at the clock. The church office would close soon. "Is Mom or Dad there?"

"No."

"No?" Tess said. "Where are they?"

"In jail," Tyler answered.

Tess controlled her temper. "This is *not* a time for joking, okay? I need to talk with them. Now."

Tyler must have heard the panic in her voice because he didn't joke anymore. "I was just kidding. Are you okay? Is everything all right?"

"Yes," Tess said. "I just need to talk with Mom or Dad." She sat back in the chair, and it squeaked.

"Okay, I'll get them. Have a good time. See you tomorrow, right?"

"Right," Tess said. She allowed a little smile to peek through her worry. Tyler was a good guy.

The phone clattered on the counter, and she could hear

Tyler calling for her parents. Soon her mother picked up another extension. "Hi, honey, how are you? Are you having a good time?"

Mom. Tess breathed a sigh of relief.

"I'm having a great time, a really great time. But I, uh, need to ask your permission for something."

"Sure," her mother said. "What is it?"

Tess sat forward in the chair, and it squeaked again. "I'd like to be baptized tomorrow. In the river. Is that okay?"

Her mother didn't answer right away. "Baptized?" she finally said. "You've never even mentioned it before."

"Well, I wanted to, but things got so busy, and there just wasn't time. And then I wasn't sure, actually," Tess rushed on. "But now I am. So can I?"

She could hear her mother exhale into the phone. "This is something I need to talk about with Dad. Let's have him on the other extension."

"Oh," Tess said in a small voice, "he's home."

"Yes, it's Friday. He's here early to help out."

In a few seconds her dad grabbed the extension Tyler had left on the kitchen counter. "Hi, cupcake. What's up? Everything okay?"

"Yes. I was just telling Mom that I want to be baptized tomorrow. Pastor Jack is baptizing three other people in the river, and I want to do it, too. Is that okay?"

"No, I don't think so," her dad answered immediately. "A river can be dangerous, and this is the first time I've heard anything about this. We're not even sure if you'll be going back to that church for a while."

"Well, I need to talk with you about that, too," Tess raced on.

"Tess," her dad interrupted, "is that Pastor Jack around?"

Tess blinked her eyes. "Well, he's down the hall. Why?"

"I'd like to talk with him. Can you get him on the phone please?"

After gulping some air Tess prayed she wouldn't faint. Never, in her worst fears, would she have imagined her dad would say something to Pastor Jack.

"I could go and get him. I have to hang up. And the office is almost ready to close," she said. "I'm sorry if I did anything wrong."

"Don't worry, honey, I'm not angry with you," her dad said, his voice softening. "Just ask Pastor Jack to call me, okay?"

"Okay," Tess whispered.

"'Bye, Tess," her mother said. "See you tomorrow. I love you."

"I love you, too. And you, too, Dad," Tess answered.

"I love you, cupcake. Now go get Pastor Jack."

"'Bye," she said, setting down the receiver.

She opened the door into the hallway and talked with the secretary. "Will you be here in like, two minutes?"

The secretary made a little clucking noise. "Not much longer. Got to get home myself."

Tess raced down the hall and explained to Pastor Jack that her dad wanted to talk with him. Pastor Jack, surprisingly, didn't seem nervous at all. Tess sat with the secretary in the outer office while Pastor Jack talked with her dad. After what seemed like two and a half days instead of five minutes, he emerged from the office.

"Well?" Tess said.

"Your dad is coming up here. He's leaving late tonight,

and he'll be here first thing in the morning. He wants to talk to us in person."

"Oh. Okay," Tess said.

Dad was angry. She knew it. He was going to flip out in front of everyone—Pastor Jack, Erin, Tom, and Shannon.

"Don't worry," Jack said. "Just have a good time at the backward party tonight, and we'll both pray about it."

"I'll try," Tess said. *You wouldn't say "Don't worry" if you knew how strong my dad can be.*

Erin stood behind Tess, buttoning up Tess's shirt on her back.

"The tag is poking me in the throat," Tess complained. "It's totally uncomfortable."

"You could have worn a T-shirt," Erin reminded her. "You just thought this looked cool."

Erin had her T-shirt and shorts on backward. "So your dad is going to be here tomorrow morning, huh?"

"Yes." Tess's heart sank. "No way would he be coming up here if he didn't think it was something important. I mean, look at the drive! And he's leaving my mom and Tyler and Tara for the day."

"You're right," Erin said. "Maybe he just wanted to see you baptized."

Tess gave her a look.

"Yeah, probably not," Erin said. "But let's just have a good time tonight, okay?"

Tess's stomach felt sick; she didn't want to eat anything. But she had been looking forward to the backward party all week; so she might as well try to have fun.

"Ready to go?" Melissa came into the room. She had a ponytail sprouting from her bangs.

"What's with that?" Erin giggled.

"Backward hairdo!" Melissa answered.

"You're crazy," Tess said.

They headed toward the dining room where, at each place setting, a plate with a piece of chocolate cake was waiting for the diner.

"I've been wanting to eat dessert first all of my life," Erin said.

Tess sat down next to her, and after they prayed—starting with the amen—they dug in.

"Let's sit by these guys." Melissa said as she and Terri plopped down across the table. "Now, try to talk backward," Melissa said.

Tess did. "Dinner after happening is what?"

"Race egg backward walking a having we're." Melissa picked her words carefully. "Movie a watching then and."

"Not from the end to the beginning, I hope!" Erin laughed.

"I need to get to bed pretty early," Tess said. Might as well blurt out the news. "My dad is coming tomorrow morning."

"Oh, Tess, how wonderful that he wants to see you get baptized." Melissa started to say something else when Erin interrupted.

"Is anyone else hungry for the real meal? I think Tess and I will go to see if dinner is ready. And then salads are last, right?" She stood up and scooted her cake plate aside.

"Don't forget to walk backward," Melissa reminded them,

laughing with the rest of the table as Tess and Erin turned their heads, looking over their shoulders, and stumbled backward toward the kitchen.

"Thanks for getting me out of that conversation," Tess said.

Erin put her arm around her friend. "I only wish I could do more."

Tess's stomach hurt. "Me, too."

fifteen

The Meeting

Saturday Morning, August 9

Tess awoke before the sun rose and tiptoed down the hall. She peeked out the front window, expecting to see her dad's Jeep parked in front. But it wasn't there yet. A cold fog rose from the ground, eerie in the moonlight. She tiptoed back down the hall and returned to her sleeping bag for another hour or two.

"Hey, wake up." Erin gently shook Tess. "It's breakfast time. Maybe your dad is here."

The room was bright with sunlight when Tess opened her eyes. She rolled over, her hair falling into her face. She struggled to sit up. "I just checked a little while ago, and he wasn't."

Melissa's sleeping bag was already rolled up.

"Today's the day!" Melissa announced. Tess watched Melissa put on her bathing suit underneath her T-shirt and shorts. Glancing at her own open suitcase, Tess saw her bathing suit strewn across a stash of clothing.

"Baptism! I'm both excited and nervous. Are you nervous?" Melissa asked Tess.

"More than you can imagine," Tess said. She dressed—without the bathing suit—and she and Erin packed up their sleeping bags. Then Tess pulled her hair back into a short ponytail and headed down to the cafeteria with Erin.

When Tess walked in, she saw her dad. He was sitting at a table, drinking coffee with Pastor Jack.

Like oil and water, the mixed-up concoction of pleasure and pain ran through Tess's heart. It was so good to see her dad. But his being here meant there was trouble.

"Hi, Dad." She kissed his cheek.

"Hi, honey." He hugged her from the side.

Tess drew a chair next to his. "When did you get here?"

"Just a few minutes ago." Her dad tilted his mug and swallowed the residue in the bottom. "Jack was kind enough to find a cup of coffee for me. It was a long drive."

"I'll get us some breakfast," Erin said. "Would you like something?" she asked Tess's dad.

"No thanks."

Erin walked toward the kitchen door.

"I know it was a long drive. You didn't have to come," Tess said.

Her dad looked straight into her eyes. "I think it's very important that I came."

"I need to go and make sure things are ready for the baptism," Jack said. "We're starting in about an hour. I'll meet the two of you in the sanctuary in twenty minutes." He picked up his paper plate, and Tess's dad nodded to him as he left the room.

"Is everything okay?" Tess asked.

"Yes," her dad answered. "We just need to talk about a few things with Jack present."

"Here's some breakfast." Erin walked back to the table

carrying two plates of scrambled eggs, bacon, and buttered toast. She set one down in front of Tess.

"Is everyone okay at home?" Tess tried to make casual conversation.

"Yep. We're all looking forward to your coming home. We've missed you." Tess ripped the fatty ribbon off her bacon and pushed the fat to the side of her plate, crunching the thin meat section. *Better get some energy.* She salted the rubbery balls of scrambled eggs and ate them, too.

Her dad checked his watch. "Shall we go?"

Tess swallowed. "Okay."

"I'll meet you in the room in a little bit, all right?" Erin said. Tess locked eyes with her, willing Erin to pray for her while she was gone.

When they arrived at the sanctuary, Pastor Jack was sitting in a pew. Her dad looked every bit as awkward in this church as he did in her church at home. They sat down next to Jack.

"I suppose you wonder why I'm here," her dad started.

"Yes...," Pastor Jack said.

"I didn't want you to get baptized without permission, Tess."

"Dad, I would never do that. I can't believe you would think that!"

"I know that now." Her dad looked a little embarrassed. "I had a good long time to think about it on the way over. And I realized that you wouldn't do that. Maybe I overreacted. It's just that when you're at church and your mother and I aren't, you're out of our control. That doesn't feel good to a parent."

He patted her hand as if to tell her he trusted her. "I guess I'm not opposed to your being a Christian, since there doesn't seem to be much I can do about it anyway. But I wanted to make sure that, because I'm not at church and Jack is, he understands my position. And I'm not comfortable with your going to church without the Janssens."

Tess spoke up. "I asked my friend Melissa if she would take me every Sunday. She said yes. Her parents are here. Hey, you could meet them. Maybe that would make you feel better."

Her dad nodded but didn't smile. "So what's this baptism thing about?"

All the answers she had jotted down on her questionnaire flooded back. "Well, when you're baptized you're telling the whole world, publicly, that you're a Christian. That you're standing up for Jesus like he stands up for you. And I just kept feeling like God wanted me to do it now. You always say the time to obey is when you're told to do it," she said, grinning.

Her dad seemed as if he couldn't help it; he grinned back.

"Being a Christian won't make me overinvolved with church, Dad. It hasn't changed me for the worse, has it?"

"No," her dad admitted. "If anything, you've grown more tender-hearted and trustworthy in the last year."

Pastor Jack said nothing, letting the two of them talk it out.

"So can I still go to church? I promise it won't interfere with school or family."

Tess's dad turned toward Jack. "You're there each week, overseeing the junior-high area?"

"Yes," Pastor Jack said. "And when I'm not, perhaps Melissa's parents will take Tess under their wing."

Tess's dad said nothing, stroking the stubble on his chin left over from his all-night drive. "Okay."

Silence slipped by as they sat together.

"And can I get baptized today?" Tess finally asked.

No one spoke for a minute. Tess's father finally sighed. "I suppose. Since I'm here now."

"Thanks, Daddy!" Tess threw her arms around her father. "I knew you would understand."

"Actually, Tess, I don't understand why you want to be baptized. But I do understand that you're a loving and responsible girl. So I'll give my okay."

He stood up. "I'm going to use the men's room, and I'll meet you in front of the church."

"Thanks, Dad."

That left just Tess and Pastor Jack. Tess grinned, and Pastor Jack grinned with her.

"That wasn't easy, was it?" he asked.

"No." Tess clasped her hands together to stop them from shaking. "But I've never been the kind of girl who is afraid of difficult things." She smiled to herself. "I need to put on my bathing suit. But I'm glad my dad left because I need to ask you one more important thing."

sixteen

Into the River

Saturday, August 9

"Sure, Tess, what is it?" Pastor Jack asked as he shifted his position on the church pew.

"Well, you know how everyone else has family here to stand by them at the river? Family that's supposed to stand by them and encourage their Christian life?"

"Yes."

Tess unclasped her hands. "I don't have any Christian family. I don't want my dad to feel embarrassed. He'll see that all the other kids who are being baptized have their family down next to the river, waiting for them to walk out, so he'll do it, too. I just want to make sure that you're not going to say anything that would make him feel weird."

Jack smiled. "I'll be really sensitive." He looked at his watch. "You had better go change, and I'd better get everyone else to the river. Meet us there with your dad, okay?"

"Okay." Tess raced back to her room and spilled out all the details to Erin.

"Yippee!" Erin said. "You're getting baptized; you did it!"

The two of them danced around the room in glee, holding hands.

"I'd better get down to the river with everyone else," Erin said. "I'll save a place for you and your dad."

"Thanks."

After Erin left, Tess wriggled into her bathing suit and pulled on her cover-up over it.

"Into the river, Jesus," she whispered to the cross on a child's picture hanging on the wall. "Just like you."

She walked down the hall and met her dad, who was waiting for her in the now deserted church.

"Ready?" she asked.

"Ready," he answered. Together they walked across the dusty path to the riverbank and then over it, to where the rest of the group waited.

Erin and Tom had saved a smooth rock near the ones they sat on. Tess sat, but her dad stood. She listened to the birds' sweet chirping in the barely stirring air around her.

Eleanor and Roshanna walked over, and Roshanna held out Tess's baptismal robe to her. "Here's your robe. I wanted to give it to you."

Tess slipped out of her cover-up and into the robe and hugged the little girl. Then Tess hugged Eleanor.

"You'll never look more beautiful than you do today," Eleanor whispered into Tess's ear before she and Roshanna left to sit down nearby. Tess squeezed back the tears. First Paul went forward. He walked straight into the water without looking back. That's how Pastor Jack had told them to do it—straight out without looking back, like they were supposed to do once they decided to follow Christ. Paul's mom and dad stood at the river as he splashed in and then as Pastor Jack dunked him all the way under. Tess tried to hear what Pastor Jack was saying to Paul but couldn't hear anything.

Afterward, Paul turned around, and everyone clapped and whistled as his dad wrapped him in a big towel. The two of them walked back to sit down on the rocks with the rest of the crowd.

Next went Jamie.

"Hey, whatever happened to girls first," Erin whispered.

Tess giggled, glad for her nearby friend's warmth. Jamie walked down to the river without looking back, the hem of his baptismal robe blowing in the light morning wind.

Jamie listened as Pastor Jack spoke to him and then was dunked completely under the water. As he rose, the crowd clapped and whistled. Jamie's mom and his two brothers stood at the side of the river, waiting for him to come out. They wrapped him in a big warm towel as Melissa went forward.

While Melissa made her way to the water's edge, Tess whispered to her father, who had joined her on the rock, "That's Melissa. You know, the one I told you about?"

Her dad nodded and put his arm around her.

Tess glanced at the nearby cross. Her name was still tacked on, just where she had put it yesterday. *Yesterday I had no idea how this was going to turn out. Amazing.*

Melissa walked into the water, and Tess watched. Melissa's mom and dad stood at the water's edge. Her little sister had stayed home with their grandparents.

When Melissa came out, everyone clapped and cheered as she walked back to shore.

"Your turn," Erin whispered.

When Tess tried to stand up, her legs felt full of holes, as if her bones were sponge and she might fall over.

"Do you want some help?" Erin asked.

"No, I can stand."

Tess walked toward the river, never looking back. She stepped into the icy water, all gray and brown and orange with silt from the reservation's sand. The water weighed down the robe, and moving her feet forward was harder with each step. She kept walking toward Pastor Jack.

When she reached him, he spoke. "You've chosen to bury your old life, to die to sin and its power. When I hold you under the water, that symbolizes your death, with Christ, to those things. And when I lift you up, it symbolizes your rising to a new life, like Christ."

Tess shivered, but not from the cold. She felt Pastor Jack's hands behind her back, and she closed her eyes.

Here I come, Lord. She first felt the back of her head and then her whole body descend under water.

And now I rise.

Jack lifted her up, and Tess turned around. She had expected to see her dad waiting alone for her at the river's edge. And she did see him, but he wasn't alone. Erin stood beside him, smiling and blinking back her own tears.

In spite of the chill, a syrupy warmth spread through Tess's heart. She looked back at Pastor Jack, who smiled knowingly.

Tess's throat felt thick with tears, tears that escaped and then mingled with river water on her face as she slowly made her way back to the river's edge. Pastor Jack supported her as she stumbled toward the shore.

Her dad held out a towel. After wrapping her in it, he held her close for a long time.

Next Tess hugged Erin, who hugged her back. Tightly.

"See?" Erin whispered as she pulled back. "You do have Christian family to stick with you no matter what. Everyone here." She motioned toward the crowd gathered. "And especially me."

Erin put her arm around Tess's shoulder. "Secret Sisters forever?"

Tess put her arm around Erin and smiled. "Of course. Secret Sisters forever."

Have More Fun!!

Visit the official website at:
www.secretsisters.com

There are lots of activities and exciting new things to see!
If you don't have access to the Internet, please write to
me at:

Sandra Byrd
P.O. Box 2115
Gresham, OR 97030

Would you like to own your own Secret Sisters charms?
You can buy a set that includes each of the eight silver
charms Tess and Erin own—a heart, ponies, star, angel,
Bible, paintbrush, dolphin, and flower bouquet. Please
send $8 (includes shipping and handling) to: Parables
Charms, P.O. Box 2115, Gresham, OR 97030. Quantities
are limited.

Navajo Fry Bread

Get a parent to help you with this. The results are hot and tasty!

Sift into a bowl:
41/2 **cups flour**
1/2 **t. salt**
2 t. baking powder

Stir in:
11/2 **cups water**
1/2 **cup milk**

Knead well with your hands, till smooth and stretchy. Pat into five-inch circles as thick as a thick pancake. Fry in several inches of hot oil at 400 degrees (test with candy thermometer or use electric frying pan). Dough will puff and bubble. Turn when golden brown. Drain on paper towel, and when cooled drizzle with a bit of honey or serve with beans, ground beef, cheese, and tomatoes to make Navajo tacos. Serves 6.

Have you read every book? Answer yes or no.
Then solve these clues to see what you know.

Across

4 Tess had a disaster with these flowers in Book 8

5 Tess's rival in Book 10

9 The beverage Tess and her mother had at their special lunch in Book 1

11 What Tess and Erin want to do in Book 11

12 Pastor Jack tossed a fake one of these into the audience in Book 2

Down

1 Tess's Navajo little sister in Book 12

2 The sport in which Tess wanted to compete during Book 5

3 Where the Secret Sisters went on vacation in Book 7

6 Where Tess had to tell all to the entire sixth grade in Book 9

7 The name of Erin's sick horse in Book 3

8 What was missing from Tess's nativity set in Book 4

10 What Tess and Erin had to wash in Book 6, even though Tess didn't want to at first

#8 *Petal Power:* Ms. Martinez is the most beautiful bride in the world, and the sisters are there to help her get married. When trouble strikes her honeymoon plans, Tess and Erin must find a way to help save them.

#9 *First Place:* The Coronado Club insists Tess won't be able to hike across the Grand Canyon and plans to tell the whole sixth grade about it at Outdoor School. Tess looks confident but worries in silence, not wanting to share the secret that could lead to disaster.

#10 *Camp Cowgirl:* The Secret Sisters are ready for an awesome summer camp at a Tucson horse ranch, until something—and someone—interferes. What happens if your best friend wants other friends, and you're not sure, but you might too?

#11 *Picture Perfect:* Tess and Erin sign up for modeling school, but will they be able to go? Could they ever get any modeling assignments? Along the way the Secret Sisters find out that things aren't always just as they seem, a fact confirmed when Tess's mother has her baby.

#12 *Indian Summer:* When Tess and Erin sign up to go on their first mission trip—to the Navajo reservation—they plan to work at Vacation Bible School. What do a young Navajo girl and Tess have in common? In the end Tess has to make some of the most important choices in her new Christian life.

The Secret Sister Handbook: 101 Cool Ideas for You and Your Best Friend! It's fun to read about Tess and Erin and just as fun to do things with your own Secret Sister! This book is jam-packed with great things for you to do together all year long.